love alive in our hearts

Mignon

Mignon C. Reynolds

Life as Bonkers

Max Limited

PORTLAND • OREGON

Cover illustration
by
Aaron J. Reynolds

Published in the United States
by
Max Limited
Portland, Oregon

Second Edition

Library of Congress, Copyright Office
Registration Number TXu 1-059-068
Certificate issued in accordance
with title 17, United States Code

Printed in the United States of America

Contents

For my son, Aaron, who showed
me how to see with kindness.

I. A New Home

It was a warm, sunny, late-summer day, the kind that left a taste of bittersweet orange in the back of the throat and sunspots jumping in front of the eyes. It was a day for skipping stones on the river, or eating popcorn in the tree house, or hiking into the cool, dense woods and finding crawdads in the stream. It was a day when the leaves were still green and the breeze was still warm. It was a day of a precious discovery; it was on this day that Curtis James found a puppy beneath a fern frond in the backyard woods.

She was a cute puppy, as all puppies are, and very tiny. She was black, with a small white star on her chest and one white paw. She was cuddly and warm, and when the boy picked her up, she seemed to go right to sleep in his arms. He walked slowly and carefully as he carried her toward the house, and he rang the bell so he wouldn't drop her while turning the knob. His mother came to open the door. She gently took the sleeping puppy and cradled it in her arms.

"Mom, isn't she wonderful?" said Curtis James quietly.

"Yes," she said, smiling. "Wonderful." She felt the puppy's warm, soft fur with her cheek and then carefully handed her back to her son. She made up a basket with a soft, cozy blanket and placed it in the kitchen, into which Curtis James put the puppy.

"Well, what's this?" asked Curtis James' father as he entered the kitchen. He walked over to the basket and bent over it to get a good look. The puppy's nose popped out, and her pink tongue gave him a lick on the nose. He laughed, and looked up at the expectant faces of his wife and his son.

"It appears we have a new member of the family," he said.

Curtis James jumped into the air and whooped. For most of his short life, he had wanted a little brother, or even a sister; he got lonely at times, being an only child. A dog would probably be even better.

The puppy slept for most of the first day, but her calmness was decidedly short-lived. The following day and every day since, she popped up from the basket with a jump and a scurry and a leap and a charge. She quickly found a place in the hearts of the people. She liked to play, although like any puppy, she sometimes forgot that her teeth were razor sharp or that not everybody wanted to be jumped upon with muddy paws. However, she was good-natured, very affectionate, and eager to please her people. She soon came to know them by the names Curtis James, MomSarah, and JoelDad.

"We need to name her," said JoelDad.

"But what?" asked Curtis James. The puppy rolled onto her back and as she did so, untied his shoelaces with her teeth. Then she popped up and ran as fast as she could, not exactly looking where she was going. Curtis James attempted to take chase, but he tripped over an untied shoelace and landed with a poof-thud onto a large pillow. The puppy zoomed around behind him like a blue-hot streak of lightning and ran smack into the low coffee table. That did not stop her. She put her tail down close to the floor and ran as fast as she could from one end of the house to the other. She looked like a black blur being led by frantically bobbing white teeth. Just as Curtis James was attempting to stand up, she ran under his feet and knocked him off them again. MomSarah and JoelDad stood laughing.

"That dog is nuts," said JoelDad. "Look in her eyes—she has a kind of goofy-fun streak. Wild and crazy."

"She might be hurt," said MomSarah with concern. "She did bonk her head." Luckily the coffee table had rounded edges, and the puppy didn't seem to act hurt.

"That's it!" shouted Curtis James. "We should call her Bonkers." The puppy ran into the middle of them, jumped into the air and fell into a clumsy back flip, skittered to her feet, and tore into the kitchen. The people looked after her, laughing, and they all agreed that Bonkers was a good name for a fun-loving, slightly nutty puppy.

That was how Bonkers earned her name, and that was how the people who had found her became her family. A dog who is given a name by people is a dog who has been adopted into their home.

JoelDad built Bonkers a sheltered and comfortable house just outside the back door, but when she was sent there at bedtime, she just cried and scratched at the door until a very sleepy person finally let her in. She was put in her cozy basket in the kitchen after that, where she remained quiet, for fear of being sent outdoors again. Being silent, however, did not stop her eyes from observing or her mind from devising a plan. She loved all her people very much, and desperately wanted to be with them, especially Curtis James, who was her favorite person in the family. She needed to get past that kitchen door. One night, she noticed that an apron string had slid into the crack on the hinged side of the closing door—just maybe it had kept the door from completely latching. She waited until the house was dark and quiet, and she padded softly to the door. Sure enough, after just a little push it opened, and she quickly and silently scurried to Curtis James' room.

When MomSarah went to wake Curtis James in the morning, she saw not only the usual sandy-brown hair of her son on the pillow, but also shiny black with a-little-bit-of-white fur next to it. She didn't wake them, but went to get her camera and took a picture. Then she gently picked up Bonkers and returned her to her basket in the kitchen.

Being shut in the kitchen at night could no longer stop Bonkers; she had figured out she could use her nose to slide the apron string into the crack just as the door was closing. The next night she was out again, and the night after that. She could not be kept out of her boy's room. She soon discovered she would not immediately be sent back to the kitchen if she stayed out of the boy's bed. It didn't matter to Bonkers that she usually had to sleep on top of a jumble of plastic toys and books left beside the bed; she just nestled in and created a snug place. She was always there to lick Curtis James' face when he woke. Eventually, MomSarah came to leave a softly worn blanket beside the bed, and Bonkers curled up happily beside her boy every night.

Fall arrived, and along with its shorter and cooler days came the loneliness of waiting for Curtis James to come home from school. The house seemed very empty and quiet to Bonkers without her boy, although it wasn't so bad when she was in the kitchen. That particular room was a wonderful place for a dog. In addition to providing her with her favorite warm spot in front of the refrigerator, it was the ultimate provider of olfactory sensation. It was pleasantly mouth-watering to be there when MomSarah made a roast chicken, or when JoelDad cooked marinara sauce.

In fact, the kitchen always smelled delectable to a dog, even when the humans thought quite the opposite. It smelled of popcorn, cheese and eggs, bacon fat, and sweet basil. There was the aroma of coffee, pepper-ham, and chocolate chip cookies. Behind the stove, it smelled of spilt creamy milk, garlic, and savory gristle. Bonkers could find slipped-into-the-cracks and wedged-under-cabinet treats, such as apple peels and kicked-under pieces of candy. There were always crumbs in plain sight, such as bits of crackers, chips, and banana nut muffins. In the kitchen, aromas old and new stimulated her keen sense of smell: pizza and blueberry pie and dog bones and simmering beef stew and savory broth and pancakes and butter smeared by small fingers under the table and fresh grapes and lamb chops and churning ice cream.

But none of these fine scents could compare with the best-of-all-to-a-dog, elusive-but-yet-all-pervasive smell of garbage in the can. This tantalizing aroma at times lured Bonkers into garbage-can trouble, the result of which ended in her being sent brusquely outside.

Being outdoors didn't bother Bonkers; it was just fine as long as it wasn't raining. She loved the smells and sights of fall, the bright colors of the leaves, and the crisp, cool air. It was perfect for chasing after squirrels, although she never caught any. It was also perfect for rolling in the dirt. The only problem she had was that she was usually given a bath afterward, especially if she had acquired bits of rotten peaches in her fur. She was usually quite proud of the aroma she achieved after a good roll, but JoelDad and MomSarah did not see it the same way and promptly removed her doggie perfume.

Bonkers' favorite time was on weekends, when she could run, make noise, and chase balls with Curtis James. She was getting bigger and could run very fast after balls, but she was too proud to bring them back. Her boy didn't mind that she didn't retrieve and happily ran to pick them up. After he tired of all the running, the boy shifted his attention to his favorite games, which were those of adventure and imagination.

"Arrrgh!" he shouted, jumping like an explosion out of a leaf pile, wearing a pirate's knotted scarf and eye patch, while brandishing a stick. "Avast ye matey. Look alive, ya mangy scalawag!"

Bonkers, taking mock offense at being called mangy, jumped up in the air to grab the stick out of Curtis James' hand and ran off with it. The boy ran after her, scattering leaves and yelling, "Come back you yellow-bellied mongrel! A curse on ye."

JoelDad came around the corner of the house with a leaf bag just in time to see a few remaining airborne leaves fluttering to the ground as the boy and dog who had just ruined his leaf pile disappeared into the woods.

Bonkers had other moments when she was not completely well behaved. Just like any teething puppy, she liked to chew on things, to discover the feeling of new textures being torn by her teeth and sliding between her gums. She chewed up socks, plastic game pieces, MomSarah's favorite sandals, and even electrical cords if they weren't properly tucked away. But her all-time favorite chew toys were yellow rubber duckies, which she ruthlessly decapitated.

"Mom!" shouted Curtis James. "Look what Bonkers did—*again*." He held up yet another headless rubber ducky.

"Oh, Bonkers," said MomSarah, shaking her head and, although amused, trying to look angry. "What are we going to do with you?" Bonkers just sat looking at her, with innocent wide eyes.

"That's the third ducky," said Curtis James, looking with exasperation at what was left of it. He wasn't very sad, since he had long outgrown the duckies, but he did like to keep them around since they had once been his favorite toys. MomSarah tossed it into the garbage, and shut the last two duckies safely inside a high bathroom cupboard.

Winter passed quickly, with many naps by the fire atop the soft blanket Santa had brought Bonkers. Spring brought many naps by the fire as well, due to the heavy rains that were normal for spring in the rainforest. By the next summer, Bonkers had grown to become nearly her full adult size, which was neither too big nor too small. She appeared to be part spaniel, with maybe some Border collie, and a little mystery dog thrown in for good measure—a perfect mix for a good mutt. Her coat was black and shiny, and her teeth were strong and white. MomSarah laughingly called her a dog-elope when she saw how the dog bounded like a gazelle as she ran through the brush.

Every weekday afternoon at 3:07 during the long school year, Bonkers waited eagerly by the door for her boy. She jumped and did back flips when he arrived. Finally, summer vacation once again arrived, and she did her back flips beside Curtis James' bed the minute he woke up. She knew the days ahead held nothing but fun for the two of them.

One mid-summer day, Curtis James dressed with super-hero speed, ate a quick breakfast, and then he and Bonkers tumbled out the door and raced to a nearby park. They ran and played all morning, and rested under a shady tree where they ate a picnic lunch. MomSarah had as usual come along and sat nearby, reading a book, but now she was on the far side of the park, feeding the ducks.

A man, a stranger, walked up to the boy. "Can you come help me find my puppy?" he asked. He looked friendly enough, and he was holding an unattached leash. "It wandered off and I can't find it."

Curtis James wanted to help the man, but he knew he was not supposed to do some things strangers asked, like going somewhere or accepting gifts. He remembered that his mom had said most people were nice, but there were some ill-intentioned people who were just pretending. Pretending to be nice was how they could get away with doing bad things; if they acted as their true selves, they would just frighten kids away.

"Please come help me. I don't know what to do. It's such a cute little puppy, and it's very young. I need to find it and feed it," said the man.

Curtis James, worrying about the puppy, wanted to help, but he remembered his mother's words and hesitated.

"Come help, please?" the man persisted.

Bonkers went over to the man and sniffed him. She knew he was telling a lie, because she did not smell any dog or puppy odor, not even on the leash. She stood in front of her boy and bared her teeth, growling at the man.

"Whoa, now," said the man as he took a step backward. "Hey kid, what's the matter with that dog of yours?"

Bonkers, her eyes sparkling with electricity, took a step forward, growled louder, and began to bark angrily and relentlessly. MomSarah came running when she heard the furious barking. The man took a few more steps backward, holding his hand out in front of Bonkers, and then turned and ran. Bonkers took pursuit for a short distance and then returned to Curtis James. The man disappeared into the trees.

Not long after, a police officer arrived to speak to Curtis James. Bonkers at first barked with menace when she saw the uniform, but she quickly perked her ears and wagged her tail when she perceived no threat to her boy. As Curtis James told the officer what had happened, Bonkers let the big man scratch her head.

That evening, Bonkers had many belly scratches from JoelDad and treats from MomSarah. It was a warm, balmy evening, and the crickets sang loudly. The moon shone brightly and a soft breeze blew through the tops of the trees. At bedtime, Bonkers was allowed in Curtis James' bed and the dog curled up in the arms of her boy. The moonlight danced on the walls in patterns made by the branches of the tall trees. Bonkers fell asleep with the songs of the crickets dancing in her head, the cool moonlight dancing in her eyes, and the warmth of her boy surrounding her.

II. A World Inside the Mind

Bonkers soon became old enough to go out on her own, and she loved to explore the outdoors. Her family's home was on a cul-de-sac, and since there were not many cars, Bonkers was at times allowed to roam. She wandered up and down the hill, and back into the woods behind the house, where there were many good smelling aromas that got even better when she poked her nose under leaves and twigs. There were people to meet, and kids and animals to play with. She sometimes got treats, and she always got pats and kind words or nuzzles. She soon met several of the neighborhood dogs: there was Jack, the mixed-breed terrier next door; Bear, the Newfoundland up the street; Lula&Orbit, the inseparable brother and sister at the very top of the hill; Eddie, who was actually a cat but thought she was a dog; and the occasional roamer just passing through.

When Bonkers first met Jack, he greeted her by sniffing excitedly, which she did in return. Then he looked her directly in the eye and said, "Hi, pal."

Bonkers jumped straight up into the air. She had never heard a dog speak with actual words before. She looked around to see if anyone else had heard. There were humans close enough to hear, but they just kept talking without seeming to take notice of anything unusual. She turned back to Jack and answered his salutation with a friendly bark.

"A bark! Don't you know Doggle? You have to get out more. Meet other dogs." Sure enough, it was the dog who was talking.

Bonkers again looked around at the humans, but they just kept talking with each other, not paying any attention to the two dogs.

"No, humans can't perceive dog language. They just think we're playing," stated Jack. That said, he gave her ear a mischievous tug and ran off. Bonkers ran after in hot pursuit. Nobody was a match for Bonkers. She was wild and crazy, and she could run a blue streak. In no time, Jack was knocked over onto the ground with Bonkers standing over him. He looked so funny, so confused and befuddled, that Bonkers had to laugh.

"I heard that! You can laugh in Doggle! We'll have you talking in no time." Without delay, Jack started to teach her all about the dog language, called Doggle. Bonkers sat up straight and perked up her ears to listen to her first lesson.

"Okay, kid. The first thing you need to know is that there are only a few human words that are necessary. If you learn too many human words, they might put you to work in a circus or something and make you work hard for your dinner."

"Way, Shack?" said Bonkers attempting a sentence.

"Good try, kid, but it's 'why, Jack.' Now listen up pup, this is important. Tidbits and Scraps—that's all you need to know about the human language. If you learn any more it will crowd out the Doggle words."

"Why, Jack?"

"Good—now ya got it. It will crowd out Doggle, because we dogs have very big hearts, but small brains. We have unlimited kindness, but we have to be careful about how much we put into our brains, because they fill up."

"Why?"

"Because they do. Now just listen. Tidbits and Scraps. These are the only human words you need to know to get by, the ones that'll keep you out of serious trouble or earn you treats—words like 'sit' and 'stay.' If you learn any more human words, you won't have enough room for Doggle, which most canines find far more useful and interesting."

"Why?"

"Puh-*lease* stop asking why! Now here are the most important Tidbits and Scraps: dinnertime, walk, stay, sit, come, and, of course, your name. Forget the rest—even if you understand something like 'quiet,' just ignore their commands like I do. Give 'em big puppy eyes afterwards and they'll be happy again. Humans seem to like it if you just *try* to please them, no matter if you get it right or not. Oh, and when in doubt—sit."

"Jack?"

"Yes?"

"Why?"

"Aaaaaaargh! No more whys! What are you, a tiny pup with her eyes still closed?"

"No, I'm Bonkers!"

"Good girl. Now you're talking," he said. "Okay. Now you know *who* you are, you must learn *where* you are. You live next to the Woods-in-the-Back, near to the Big Forest. All of this is just a small part of our planet, Dirt."

"Dirt?" said Bonkers, thinking about the name.

"Yes, Dirt," Jack repeated. "That's what it's made of, isn't it?"

Bonkers dug in the ground a bit and took a good sniff. "Yes," she said. It was definitely made of dirt. She took a good long look at her surroundings, at the trees and the hills and the houses. Somehow, with words it all seemed new and different.

An intense desire to learn consumed Bonkers for the next few months. She ran out to meet Jack for lessons as often as she could. She even went out in the normally detested cold and rain, braving clammy, matted fur and chilled bones.

The lessons continued, and before long Bonkers was not only talking like a pro, but also thinking like one. As she learned Doggle her head filled up with words, words that opened up a whole new world of thought. For the first time in her life, she could describe things to herself and ask questions of herself. Before Doggle, she had merely been able to think, *Hmmm,* as she had lain basking in the sun. Now, with her new words, she was able to expand on her thoughts in many fresh and different ways, such as: *I love the warm rays beaming upon my furry belly on a late autumn afternoon, with the cool grass underneath and the smell of warm dirt wafting through the balmy air...hmmm.*

"Hey, Jack," asked Bonkers during a lesson on dog breeds, "What happens when a dog's head fills up? I mean, when there's no more room for more words?"

"I'm not exactly sure," he replied. "I think it just gets kind of quiet for a bit while your brain takes a rest. I've heard about it from some other dogs, but it's never happened to me."

"I guess you could call it a 'Doggle boggle'."

Jack laughed. "Or a 'chock-full pit bull'."

Bonkers rolled around on the ground and popped up, saying, "No, no—wait a sec. How about this—a 'confounded hound-head'."

"Kid," laughed Jack, "you're a quick learner. You're starting to speak like a pro." Bonkers tugged on his tail and ran off into the woods, and Jack tore after her.

Bonkers soon found she could happily spend a whole day thinking and exploring the inside of her mind. She didn't need too much from the outside world, just a full belly, a place to roam, and lots of pats. Although she still immensely enjoyed running, she no longer found it necessary to race around just to escape boredom; entertainment was now provided by the thoughts racing around inside her head: *Why is the sky blue? Where do dogs come from? What happens when we die? How does the world look to the teeniest bug?*

Of course, Bonkers couldn't speak to Curtis James in Doggle, but that didn't bother her. The two communicated by sharing with each other. They shared playtime and potato chips; a warm blanket and a good book on rainy nights; homemade forts, sock fights, and towel tugs; bubble blowing (Bonkers liked to pop them); running, shouting and barking; quiet time with hugs; and, best of all, the deep bond of friendship. Bonkers knew she would do anything she could to protect her boy, even jump in front of a car or fight a large wild animal if necessary.

III. Friendships Made Richer

Jack quickly became Bonkers' best dog friend. He lived next door to her and met up with her just about every day when Curtis James was away at school. He was kind and patient. He had taught her Doggle, the fact of which made Bonkers very grateful, and he was great fun to play with. The two dogs chased each other's tails, ran races, and shared bones; they felt good together and felt bad together. They did everything together, or they did nothing together; it didn't matter what as long as they did it together.

Jack, like Bonkers, was a mutt, being a mixed-breed of part terrier and part who-knows-what. His keen sense of smell indicated he probably had inherited a bit of hound at some point. Jack was a pound dog; many years prior, he had been judged guilty of the 'crime' of being alone in the world and thrown into doggie-jail. In actuality, he had a home, but he had run far away after having been frightened by some fireworks. Despite his keen nose, he had never found his way back again. Ultimately it had ended well, since his new family, the family he now loved, had come to his rescue, releasing him from that horrible place.

"Hey, Bonkers," announced Jack one day, "it's time you were given a proper introduction to the gang."

By this time, Bonkers had come across the other dogs in the neighborhood, but she had never been formally introduced to them. In addition, she had not then been capable of joining in conversation with them due to her lack of a working knowledge of Doggle.

A slight breeze rustled overhead branches as Bonkers eagerly followed Jack down the driveway to the street. A little rat-creature that appeared to be somewhat doglike ran up to them with a yap, yip, yap! At first, Bonkers tried talking to it, but it just kept yapping at her, so she gave up. Jack didn't seem to take notice of it as he continued on his way.

"Jack, was that a dog?" asked Bonkers, when they were out of earshot.

"Yeah, that's Aldo. He doesn't know how to speak—since he's so little, his brain is way too small to learn much of anything. Sometimes I think Eddie is more of a dog than that yappy fellow," said Jack.

"Did I hear my name?" Eddie appeared from behind some bushes.

"Speaking of not-quite-dogs," whispered Jack to Bonkers, very quietly so Eddie would not hear. Eddie was one of the neighborhood cats, and she would just pop out from anywhere whenever her name was mentioned. She was no ordinary cat; she was an honorary dog, since she spoke Doggle, a feat not previously accomplished by any other cat known to the neighborhood. Cats didn't have a language, and even if one existed, they are generally too aloof to speak to each other. Eddie, being far from aloof, was more disposed to play canine games and to prefer the company of dogs rather than fellow cats.

"Hey Eddie, old pal," said Jack at full volume. "I would like to formally introduce you to my friend, Bonkers. She has recently become an accomplished speaker of Doggle."

"I am very pleased to make your acquaintance," said Bonkers to Eddie. The dog and cat had met several times previously, but during those times Bonkers had not yet been able to speak.

Eddie smiled at her. "I am very pleased as well," she said. "You're coming along quite well with your speech. What a quick study!"

"We're heading up the street in order to give Bonkers proper introductions to the gang," said Jack. "Wanta come?"

"Yeah, of course," said Eddie. "Let's go see Bear first." Bear had long been her favorite friend, since her tiny kitten days. He was a huge dog, a giant Newfoundland. His massive countenance naturally incurred fear and awe in smaller animals, but without grounds. In actuality, he was the kindest and gentlest of animals. His great size afforded him the position of protector of the neighborhood, and he took his job seriously, occupying the pavement in front of his house every day, rain or shine.

Bear was in his usual position this day, contentedly snoozing on the pavement with his head cradled in his enormous paws. Eddie took the opportunity to jump on his head and cover his eyes with her tail.

"Wake up, Bear," she said, tauntingly. "We have someone who wants to meet you."

Bear, being the massive dog he was, had huge eyes that could easily see past the skinny little tail, but he didn't let on.

"Hmmm…," he said. "I must ponder…" Jack and Bonkers remained silent, complicit in Bear's deception of Eddie.

"It's someone you know," said Eddie, "but there is something different."

"If I may conjecture," said Bear, rising and depositing Eddie on the ground as he did so, "Might it concern our young acquaintance, Bonkers? May the distinction be that she now possesses a working command of Doggle?"

"Yes, Bear, yes! I do speak Doggle," said Bonkers. "How did you know?"

"Simple cogitation and speculation," said Bear. He had guessed Bonkers would now be speaking, since she had arrived at the appropriate age. "May I inquire, as to what precipitates this assemblage of our youthful ingénue and her genteel companions?"

"Huh?" said Bonkers.

Bear had a manner of speaking that often surpassed the abilities of his companions to understand. He had lived a long life, during which he had acquired a scholarly tongue. He was a wise dog, and his life had been full of adventure and experience. Although he was getting on in years, his mind continued to be sharp and full of stories that he never hesitated to tell to young ears that were eager to learn about the world.

"Pardon me," said Bear, realizing he had verbally distanced his friends. "Why did all of you so graciously come for a visit?"

"We came," said Jack with pride in his teaching ability, "in order to formally present Bonkers to you, since she is now a good speaker of Doggle."

"Naturally," said Bear. "A most worthy rite of passage."

Turning to Bonkers, he said, "Mademoiselle, it is with the utmost pleasure and decorum that I duly make your delightful acquaintance."

"The pleasure is mine," said Bonkers, standing tall and proud. She extended her paw, and Bear quite properly licked it.

Just then, some loud barking came from up the street.

"*You* did it!" shouted an irritated voice.

"No, *you* did it!" answered another voice.

Eddie rolled her eyes and stretched. Bear yawned and once again lay down on the pavement.

"What's going on?" asked Bonkers. She recognized the arguing voices coming from atop the hill as those of Lula&Orbit, the brother and sister pups who were always together.

"Let's go see," said Jack, always ready for an adventure.

"I'll stay here," said Eddie, licking her paw with disinterest.

"I shall remain as well," said Bear. "It is imperative that I retain my station."

"Come on," said Jack. "Let's go!" He and Bonkers ran up the street, in the direction of the barking.

"Hey, Jack!" said Lula, with her customary frenzy, as soon as she saw him.

"Howl-dy, Bonkers!" said Orbit, with just as much excitement in his voice.

"We were just arguing about...," Lula hesitated. "Um...about...oh, I forgot. What *were* we arguing about, Orbit?"

"Oh, never mind," he said. "Hey Bonkers! Hey Jack! There's a new stinkpile! Come roll in it with us."

"Yea—c'mon pups," said Lula. "Let's roll!"

"But I came here in order to formally introduce—," started Jack.

"Oh, nevermindthatnow," interrupted Orbit. "We have a stinkpile. Come on!"

"Whizwag!" said Bonkers, "Let's go." Lula&Orbit stopped in their tracks, taken aback by the sound of perfect Doggle coming from the mouth of Bonkers for the very first time.

"Did you hear that?" asked Lula.

"I think so," said Orbit.

"I said, let's run 'n roll," said Bonkers.

"Bowser-wowser, she speaks!" said Orbit.

"That's what I was trying to—," started Jack.

"Fantabulous, Bonkers," interrupted Lula. "Now you can yappity-yap with the rest of the gang."

"This calls for a celebration!" shouted Orbit. "Riffruff and mutts, one and all, let's roll!"

Lula&Orbit ran ahead, so fast they seemed to blur together. Jack, resigned to the fact that he was never going to be able to get more than half a word in with Lula&Orbit, followed with Bonkers in fierce pursuit. There was a fresh pile of garbage, or compost as the humans preferred to call it, behind one of the homes. The four dogs dove into it, rolled in it, tossed it up in the air, and ground it into their ears.

They kept at it, until they heard a human voice shout at them, "Hey, you mutts! Git outta there. Scram!"

The dogs tore off toward their respective homes, Lula&Orbit soon reaching the safety of their nearby residence, and Bonkers and Jack racing past them down the street.

The two friends stopped in front of Jack's house, nearly breathless, but with just enough air left in their lungs to laugh. They rolled on the ground, taking enough time to catch their breath between chuckles until they were able to speak once again. *Yes,* thought Bonkers, *Jack, above all the other dogs, is special.*

"Goodnight, Jack," said Bonkers. "It was an especially good day today." She nuzzled him to say goodnight and trotted over to her home.

Alone now, Bonkers thought about all the dog friends she had met that day; met not in the sense she had never seen them before, but in the sense she had never actually been able to speak with them until now. With Doggle, she had found a new door in her world, and it was only just beginning to open. She was learning new words every day, every minute, and as she did so, she was learning about the worlds of her friends. She sensed she would come to learn of their experiences, their loves, their knowledge, and their being.

Unfortunately, upon entering her home, she was immediately given a bath, washing away all traces of the beautiful, pungent aroma she had acquired from the stinkpile. Later that evening, as she lay on the back patio gazing at the stars, she forgot about the indignity of the bath and enjoyed the crisp breeze tickling her soft, fluffy fur.

The sky above was clear, and Bonkers lazily watched stars shoot across it in a brilliant display. Suddenly the sky lit up with an intense flash of red, and from it, just as suddenly, shot a ball of fire leading a long, flaming tail. It plummeted straight for the Woods-in-the-Back, very near to the spot in which Bonkers was now standing. She jumped back in anticipation of a huge impact. Instead, there came not a sound, only an odd and complete silence. Strange. She briskly shook her head, but still neither saw nor heard anything. All was still and dark. She decided her tired eyes were playing tricks on her and went inside to sleep.

Tomorrow will be another day, she thought with happy sleepiness, *another adventure. One to share with friends.*

IV. The Addlebrained Beagle

Early the following day, on a crisp winter morning with a fresh powder of light snow shining in the sun, Bonkers trotted next door for a visit with Jack. She heard irksome little yaps coming from across the street, to which she paid little attention.

"Mmmm, Jack," she said, inhaling deeply. "Smell the air. So fresh, so clean."

"So cool, so frosty," he added.

"So tingly, so frigid, so chilly, so nippy." Bonkers took great pleasure in practicing as many of her new words as she could bring to mind.

Jack laughed. "Just the day for tearing through the woods and leaving a trail of snow-dust and breath-fog. C'mon!"

"Yea, let's already," said Bonkers.

"Did I hear my name?" Eddie appeared from behind some bushes. Bonkers started to reply she had said 'already' rather than 'Eddie,' but quickly decided not to mention the matter since she was glad to see her friend.

"Hi, Eddie!" Bonkers ran up to her. "Wanta play tug?"

"Oh, please. I am not a little puppy," said the cat.

"How about hide-and-seek?"

"Okay, you go hide and I'll come seek. Ready? One...two... three..." Bonkers ran off into the woods, leaving tracks in the snow. Eddie found a sunny spot and curled up.

"Aren't you going to go find her?" asked Jack.

"Of course not. Hide-and-seek is for puppies. I am *not* a puppy."

"Yeah, I almost forgot for a minute."

"Hey Jack, I found some good bones in the trash can. You wanta come help me pick them clean?"

"You're on!" Jack raced away with Eddie to her place, both of them immediately forgetting about Bonkers hiding in the woods.

Bonkers tore into the woods, as fast and as far as she could. When she thought Eddie was about to finish counting, she quickly found a place to hide under a loose pile of leaves near the base of a tall cedar. She stuck only the tip of her nose out and wiggled it around until she made a hole just large enough to be able to see out. It was quiet in the woods, and she could not make out any hint of a noise indicating the approach of her friends.

Bonkers thought of the night before, when her sleepy eyes had tricked her into thinking she had seen something like a meteorite hit Dirt in the Woods-in-the-Back. She mused that the spot where the meteorite had appeared to fall was very close to the exact spot in which she now stood.

Before long, clouds appeared in the sky, and with them came new snow. It fell silently, blanketing the world with a hush. Bonkers felt a few flakes fall onto her nose, the warmth of which quickly transformed them to droplets.

Just then, she detected an unusual aroma. There was something remotely familiar about it, as if it had a place in her memory, but she couldn't quite figure out what it was. It was not highly objectionable, smelling of dog. Rather strongly of dog. Curiosity got the better of her, and she climbed out of her hiding place and shook off some leafy hangers-on. She stuck her nose up high and took a good whiff. She tracked the scent through the woods for a short way, until she neared a fern where the aroma was quite pungent. She peeked behind a large frond.

A very large, friendly looking, and, oddly enough, slightly glowing beagle popped out of the underbrush. He wagged his tail in great crazy circles and exclaimed, "Bonkers! How are ya, old pal? I haven't seenya-metya in years!"

Bonkers jumped back and stared. She had never before seen any living creature that glowed—and by the way, how did this one know her name?

Behind the beagle, partially hidden by the fern, she could see what appeared to be pieces of large stone. They were haphazardly arranged in a circular position, as if they had perhaps once comprised a kind of huge, intact egg, but were now just pieces of shell, fallen into their current positions after the egg had been broken apart from inside. *Could they have once formed a round object,* Bonkers wondered, *maybe like the meteorite I saw in the sky the night before? If that were the case, could the object have been hollow in the center? Could it have carried something?* There was no snow on the stone pieces; rather, they appeared to be wet, as if radiating warmth had melted the snow that had fallen on top of them.

The beagle clumsily and happily took a bound toward her, and she again jumped back.

"Bonkers, old pal, old chum, it's me—Max. Don't you recogknow me? I know it's been a few years—but c'mon." The beagle stood still with his tail pointed up and his head tilted to the side, with a slightly goofy and friendly look on his face.

"I—I'm sorry. You seem nice, but…," she hesitated, taking a careful look at him, "why do you glow?" She ventured forward a bit, and sniffed at the air, still remaining at least a bound away from Max.

"Glow? I don't glow…. Say…where am I?" said the glowing dog, for the first time looking around at his surroundings. "Is this the Winterland? I've always wanted to go to the Winterland."

"The Winterland? No, it's not—I've never heard of that. All the dogs call this the Woods-in-the-Back," stated Bonkers. "It's where I come from," she added proudly.

Bonkers peered underneath Max and observed that he left no paw prints, although he trod through the snow. *How odd,* she thought; *a glowing dog who recognizes me and seems to float above the ground.* "Pardon me, but you didn't answer why you glow."

"Glow? But I already toldsaid you—I don't," said Max, and as he said this, he became brighter and brighter, somewhat translucent. "I feel a bit odd," he said. "A bit puguliar." Little sparks of light seemed to float off him and disappear into the air.

"Now I have to pondentrate," he said, and he stuck his floppy ears straight up in the air and promptly his big head fell to the ground with a dull thud. Rising, he said, "I've never heard of the Woods-in-the-Back. What particlesection of the Dog Planet are we in, Bonkers?"

"Dog Planet. I've never heard of a Dog Planet. All the dogs here call our world 'Dirt.' And how do you know me?"

"What do you mean, you've never heard of the Dog Planet?" As he asked this, Max glowed very brightly, becoming nearly transparent, and zinging sparkles shot through the air around him. "Why the Dog Planet is our Mothership, the place where all us dogs come from. C'mon Bonks, ya gotta memberize—you were the head navigator. Bigwig importable job you had there."

Bonkers just stood there with a blank look on her face, watching the beagle become more and more transparent, until—poof—he was gone, invisible.

"Don't ya memberize way back in puppygarten with Miss Missy? We were best pals—we always sat together."

Bonkers could hear his voice, but she could see no sign of Max. "Max, where did you go?" she called out.

"Why, right over here." His voice was coming from the opposite direction. Bonkers turned and saw a semi-transparent Max starting to reappear.

"But Bonkers, don't you even memberize me? I'm Max. Max Einstein Beagle. Miss Missy gave me my middling name, because she said I was a beagle savant. You and I were puppies together. We were bestest pals. We started in the same class together—only you kept moving up to different classes until you gradiated from Canine College. I stayed on for a few years in puppygarten. I think Miss Missy wanted me to stay acause of she likened me."

Bonkers had heard of beagle savants. They were roughly the canine equivalent of what humans call idiot savants: beings of seemingly low intelligence who somehow, on some level, function with a high level of ability. Since dogs know that 'beagle' and 'idiot' mean approximately the same thing, they see no need for being mean or redundant by saying idiot twice. They simply say 'beagle savant' rather than 'beagle idiot savant.'

Max had now fully reappeared, and Bonkers examined his face closely. She saw friendly, somewhat goofy features, with very kind eyes. Since kindness is rated much more highly than intelligence in the dog world, Bonkers readily felt an affinity for him.

"Max, I can't say I recognize you, and I don't recall any 'Dog Planet' or 'Miss Missy' or 'Canine College' or 'Winterland' or any of those things," said Bonkers, and she watched his face sink with each word. "But you seem like a nice dog, and I would really like to be your friend."

"Timbuktu!" said Max happily. He ran in circles and then ran smack into a tree, at which point—poof—he suddenly disappeared in a shower of bright and glittering sparks.

"Max! Max, are you okay?" called out Bonkers, worried he might have been hurt. She couldn't see her newfound friend anywhere. Then, from the opposite direction, her nose detected the smell of wet dirty socks and rotten peaches.

"Of course, I'm fine. What could happenstance to me?" said Max's voice coming from the direction of the rancid, but quite pleasurable to dogs, aroma. Presently the beagle started to reappear, and Bonkers ran over to him and playfully knocked him over.

Throughout the rest of the morning and the early afternoon, the two friends played. Max had a particular advantage in some of the games, such as hide-and-seek, because he left no paw prints and he could disappear. However, Bonkers was much faster, and she had no trouble tracking down his pungent and distinctive smell. They played together as if they had played the same games for a lifetime, knowing each other's moves and traits, easily being able to judge just how to trick and confound their 'opponent.'

At times the snow fell lightly, and at times the bright winter sun shone through the clouds. It was crisp outside, but it did not feel cold to

Bonkers, whose hot breath left small puffs of steam lingering in the still air. It was almost early spring. Crocus and lily shoots pushed through the snow and the fragrant smell from the bright yellow witch hazel flowers permeated the air. Bright red berries on some of the bushes beckoned to deer that wandered in from the Big Forest to eat them. At times tiny birds in large flocks flew about, like flickering fast moving clouds sweeping low over the ground. The tips of the maple branches no longer had points that disappeared into the sky, but rather rounded button-ends that contained the buds of soon-to-emerge new leaves. The formerly rock-hard soil was now in some places soft and muddy. There was a different smell in the air, part flowery-sweet, and part rich with fresh earth.

Bonkers was so lost in her play in the woods with Max and so captured by the sights and smells of early spring that she didn't even hear the back door slam or the footsteps of her approaching boy.

"Bonkers, puppy! Where were you when I got home? Oh, never mind. Let's play." Curtis James scooped up snow into snowballs that he threw for Bonkers to chase. Max ambled onto the scene just in time for one of the snowballs to fly square at his face. However, instead of smashing into him, it sailed clean through him, leaving a few glittering sparks in its wake. It landed with a dull thud on the ground.

Curtis James didn't seem to notice the new dog standing before him, so Bonkers tugged at his sleeve and led him toward Max. She ran over to the beagle, who stood wagging his tail, or rather his tail was wagging him, and she barked. She bounded next to Max, tugged on his ear, and then jumped right over him.

"Oh, I get it. You have an imaginary friend." Curtis James laughed. "You must get lonely playing by yourself all day. Hey, Mom!" he shouted. "Bonkers has an imaginary friend—come see." The boy ran to the house to get his mother. Bonkers and Max looked quizzically at each other.

"I guess he can't see you," said Bonkers. Max glowed brightly and then turned invisible. "Now *I* can't see you. Max, where did you go?" She jumped around in the snow, trying to find his scent.

Just as MomSarah came outside with Curtis James, Bonkers saw a just-starting-to-reappear Max slip into the house through the open door behind them. She raced furiously after him past her people, reaching the closing door just in time for it to shut smartly on her nose. She scratched wildly to be let in.

"I told you she was acting nutty," said Curtis James, unable to stop laughing. MomSarah opened the door and Bonkers raced inside at full speed looking for Max. It was a cinch to find him, owing to the fact that his odor was much stronger due to its being confined to the indoor space. Bonkers sniffed him out in no time and pounced on him just as he was snuggling into her fireside pillow.

"What is that awful smell?" asked MomSarah. "Peee-uuuu. Dog, you must have rolled in something gross. You need a bath. Right now. Go, dog. To the tub. Go!"

And so, Bonkers unhappily had her bath. While she was in the tub, Max slipped outside when JoelDad opened the door to come in. Once again the house smelled fresh, and everyone was satisfied the stench had been cleaned away with Bonkers' bath. After dinner, the family relaxed around the fire. JoelDad played his guitar, MomSarah read a book, Curtis James invented things with building toys, and Bonkers napped on her pillow next to the hearth.

V. A Homeland in Dreams

A chill wind heralded the arrival of nighttime on the evening of Bonkers' first encounter with Max in the Woods-in-the-Back. As she did every night, Bonkers went out to the backyard before bed. There she found Max sitting outside the door waiting for her.

"Max, my new pal—there you are. I was worried I would never see you again."

"Without a snout, you *will* see me again. And I'm your *old* pal, not your new pal," said Max.

"I wish I could remember," said Bonkers.

"Hmm, let me workthink on that," said Max. He got an intense look in his eyes, and his ears stuck straight up in the air and quivered. Soon his big head fell to the ground with a muffled thud. His eyes glowed brightly, and he became semi-transparent.

He sprang up, spun around, and said, "Pismo Beach! I got it—when you to go to sleep tonight, you'll revisit the Dog Planet in your dreams."

"Visit in my dreams?" asked Bonkers. She looked at him with

questioning eyes. "But I don't remember ever being there. How can it exist in my dreams?"

"I don't exactually know," said Max. "But I think there is some participle of you that knows." He shook his big head and stretched his back. "Maybe you do have rememberies. I think you'll find it."

That night, as Bonkers lay at the foot of Curtis James' bed, she could see a slight glow under the window where Max lay outside. Tiny blue sparkles rose up and danced in front of her eyes. They seemed to stay inside her eyelids as she shut them and dance inside her head as she began to dream.

Bonkers traveled into the night sky. She soared away from Dirt (which, from space, really looked more as if it should be called 'Water'), past a smaller red planet, and past a great giant of a planet. Suddenly, she sped up to whip past several more planets, zooming away from the rapidly shrinking sun, leaving her solar system behind as she time-traveled out to deep space. Stars appeared to be blurs as she whipped past, bearing straight ahead to the one star that was brighter than any other.

She traveled into the solar system of this star, slowing as she descended into the atmosphere of a beautiful planet. She saw snow-capped mountains, deep blue oceans, white-sand beaches, and wide green fields. This was a different world from Dirt, and yet something about it was familiar to Bonkers. She took a good sniff of the air. Yes, she recognized it; she had been here before—even lived here before. She knew it; this was the Dog Planet. This was the Mothership, her first home, the original home of all dogs.

The outer reaches of the planet suddenly became hazy and dissolved around her, and her surroundings now formed anew, transforming into an indoor room. She recognized where she now was—in her puppygarten class. She saw her best friend, Max, as a young beagle, sitting at a desk next to her. She was in a room full of young pups learning their Doggle ABC's. At the front of the room stood a kindly teacher whom she recognized as Miss Missy. Suddenly the time shifted, and it was graduation day from puppygarten. Bonkers stood with her certificate proudly displayed around her neck, while Miss Missy spoke to Max.

"Max, I want you to come back to my class next year," said Miss Missy. "Even though you don't grasp certain concepts, I can see something very wise and special inside of you. You belong in school, not in a work crew." Dogs on the Dog Planet knew that those who had difficulty learning in school ended up being sent to labor for their living.

"Aw, shucks," said a blushing Max puppy.

"Besides," continued Miss Missy, "I want you here because you have the biggest heart of any dog I have ever known. It makes me happy to have you here."

Max, turned red with embarrassment, spun in a circle, and attempted to hide his too-large-for-hiding muzzle in his paws.

Suddenly, the puppygarten room and the dogs in it dissolved around Bonkers, disappearing and then reforming into new scenes: Bonkers was in primary school—dissolve—upper school—dissolve—college—dissolve—graduation—dissolve—the control room of the Mothership. It was in the control room that her surroundings ceased to dissolve and her dizzying journey ended.

The Dog Planet was not merely a planet; it was the Mothership, a large starship that appeared on the exterior to be a planet but on the interior proved to be a huge interstellar craft, run and operated by dogs. Capable of leaving its orbit and traveling beyond its solar system, it often explored the far reaches of space. Bonkers had an important purpose in the control room: she was the head navigator of the Mothership. She wore a pin on her collar that proudly displayed her rank, an official gold pin with the insignia of a dog peering out to the stars through a sextant.

Standing at her post, Bonkers now found herself speaking: "Captain Sirius, sir, it is thirteen hundred hours. Time for my relief."

"Affirmative," responded Sirius, the alpha dog and commander of the ship, speaking in a loud voice that resonated clearly throughout the control room. As Bonkers walked by him, he lowered his voice and said quietly so only she could hear, "So tell me, are you gonna waste your time again hanging out with that goofy beagle friend of yours? Honestly, I don't know what you see in him."

Ignoring his words, Bonkers raced off to a nearby park to play with her lifelong best friend, Max. Max had never actually graduated from puppygarten, but year after year he had been invited back. Since the two friends had taken different paths in their lives, they met whenever they could: recess, break time, dinnertime, weekends.

Bonkers and Max romped in the park, hiding behind bushes and tearing across the lawn, causing ducks to take flight in alarm. While they were playing, the park suddenly dissolved around them, and their surroundings were replaced by a snowy forest in Winterland. Max ran toward Bonkers, stopped short, and sprayed her in the face with snow, obscuring her vision. As she shook it off, she noticed that somehow it was no longer cold snow, but had changed to hot sand. They were now in Summerland, playing on a sandy beach next to a bright aquamarine ocean.

The two friends continued playing as their world around them continued shifting, changing in time and place. Next they were in Dinnerland gnawing on bones that were bigger than they were; next Chaseitland, tearing along the ground after squirrels that ran atop fences; next Rollingland, rolling in piles of old garbage; next Slumberland, lying exhausted on fluffy feather pillows.

As Bonkers was falling asleep, the world of the Dog Planet appeared to liquefy and shimmer as it slowly disappeared. She heard the voice of Miss Missy, and she opened her eyes with great effort to see her favorite teacher standing before her.

"All dogs are born good dogs," said Miss Missy. "But not all dogs are born with big hearts. A big heart carries a special wisdom."

The words floated inside Bonkers' head as she was finally compelled to shut her heavy eyelids.

When Bonkers next opened her eyes, she was occupying her bed pillow at the foot of Curtis James' bed. She lay there for a while, looking at the familiar surroundings and turning the fantastic revelations of her dream over in her mind. She now knew that she had come from some place infinitely greater than just a spot underneath a fern frond in the Woods-in-the-Back. She had a history and a purpose. She was not quite sure what the purpose was, but she could feel something strong inside of her. She knew she had a homeland that she could visit in her dreams and in her memories.

Bonkers jumped up from her pillow and licked her boy's face to wake him. After Curtis James woke up laughing (he was a very good-natured child, and was always polite and cheerful upon waking), Bonkers grabbed his pajama sleeve and tugged him out of bed. While he was dressing, Bonkers ran down the hallway and scurried back with his jacket. As he put it on, she tugged at the jacket, pulling him toward the door.

"Wait, girl, wait," he said, standing his ground. "I have to get my shoes on." He put them on as quickly as he could and opened the door. Bonkers tore outside. The snow had melted overnight, and the soft morning sun glistened through bare, wet tree branches.

Bonkers ran ahead yelling, "Max, Max! I remember! I remember!"

Curtis James laughed happily as he watched Bonkers jumping, bounding, and playing with her imaginary friend.

VI. To Believe and to See

Bonkers and Max ran up the street looking for Jack. It was a sunny day, the recent dusting of snow had melted, and fresh air beckoned with a hint of jasmine and newly thawed soil. Spring called to the dogs and lured them to places anew.

"Jack! Hey, Jack!" called out Bonkers. "Noses up! I brought my oldest pal for you to meet." Max was lagging behind the swift spaniel. "Hurry your tail, Max. Come and meet Jack, my best pal from next door."

Jack had been busy sniffing out the trail of something in the underbrush when Bonkers approached. He lifted his head and greeted Bonkers, ready to meet her friend.

"Hey there, Bonkers. Any pal of yours, I'm sure, will be a pal o' mine."

Max caught up to Bonkers and put his most pleasant expression on his face, with big eyes and wide mouth. He liked Jack the instant he saw him, and immediately lay upon the ground, presenting his belly to his new acquaintance.

"Max, *what* are you doing?" whispered the horrified Bonkers down to her friend. Max was blatantly displaying he was less than equal to his new acquaintance, no better than a servant. "Get up at once, and present yourself properly!"

Max quickly stood, turned aside to Bonkers, and said quietly, "Sorry. Just a standing habit—um, no wait—a lying down habit—after so many years in puppygarten. Bottom of the barking order, y'know."

Max had a brisk shake from nose to tail, and resumed his friendly stance and countenance. He faced Jack with confidence and stated, "I am very pleased to greet with you."

"Uh...Bonkers...," said Jack with a puzzled look, "who are you speaking to? I don't see anyone."

Bonkers looked at her two friends, both of whom she could plainly see, and asked Jack, "You don't see anyone?"

"Nope. Not anybody," he replied, sniffing the air. "But I do *smell* something. Rather strong. An odor of rotten peaches," Jack paused to sniff more, "and beagle—yes, those beagles have an unmistakable aroma," sniff, sniff, "and old eggs...and sun-wilted seaweed...," sniff, "and...and...yes, some dandelion greens." Jack had an unerring nose, capable of detecting even the most minute or timeworn aroma.

"Wow, he's good," said Max to Bonkers. "A superable nose your pal there has."

"But you *see* nothing?" asked Bonkers of Jack. "Nobody there?"

"Absolutely, positively not a soul," said Jack. "Look at the ground— no paw prints in the morning dew, except for yours and mine. Sorry pal," he said and walked over to the sunny pavement to lie down, leaving Bonkers alone with Max.

"Wow. Those things he smelled are all the things I rememberize doing last on the Dog Planet," stated Max. He became oblivious to his surroundings as his recollections engulfed his attention. "First I rolled in rottened peaches...yeah, that's what I did...and then I went to Summerland and rolled in the seaslime grass. Later I ate all those putrific eggs—they were yummelicious...oh, but afterwards I got a tummyache. So I ate my greens to help—but they didn't help, just seemed to make me greensick. My tummyache got pretty bad. Yup, that's the last thing I memberize from home—that ickygross tummyache..."

Max, paused to think deeply, and as he did so, he began to sparkle and glow. "Later on I felt better, but I found I was rat-trapped inside of something. It was hot...and it moved like I was flinged through space a long ways...then I was waking up...and then there was you—my old pal." Max, now glowing and sparkling, looked happily at Bonkers, but then he grew quiet and furrowed his brow. "And the world was...oddballish...strange. It wasn't the Dog Planet anymore. Not home." He looked at Bonkers, and he looked at the world around him. He glowed very brightly, and then he started becoming transparent. "Hey, Bonkers, you don't expose that I was sent—," he started to say, but before he could finish—poof—he disappeared in a shower of zinging sparkles.

"Max? Max, where did you go?" called out Bonkers.

"Um, Bonkers?" interjected Jack, lifting his groggy head from the pavement to give her a quizzical look.

"Okay, okay, I got it already," she said with resignation. "So you can't see him."

"See—no," said Jack, lifting his nose to sniff the air, "but I can definitely smell something."

I stink; therefore I am, thought Max, sitting behind some nearby bushes, listening to the conversation. *How odd that he can't see me,* thought the beagle. *Maybe I just haven't made myself noticeable enough to him yet. Maybe if I try harder.* Max got an idea and ran off, sparks flying in his wake.

"Bonkers," said Jack kindly, "come here and tell me about your old friend."

"Well, he and I have been best friends for a long time, from way back when we were puppies on the Dog Planet. We did everything together."

"The Dog Planet! Why I haven't talked about that old place in quite a while. Do you believe in it, Bonkers?"

"Well, yes of course," said Bonkers, who no longer had even a smidgen of doubt since her dream. "Don't you?"

"Yeah, sure. I used to believe in it. When I was a pup. But that was when I was a pup."

Just then, Max flashed by in a shower of sparks, zooming down the hill while sitting on a skateboard. Bonkers laughed, but Jack didn't seem to notice the beagle.

"What's so funny?" asked Jack.

"Didn't you see?"

"What, the Dog Planet?" asked Jack, who had been completely oblivious to Max's display. "No, of course not. It's not real, Bonkers. It's only the stuff of dreams."

Max zoomed by on the skateboard again, this time standing uncertainly on only his back paws, like a human man trying to stand in ladies' high heels. Bonkers doubled over in laughter, falling onto the ground.

"What's so funny about dreams?" asked Jack with indignation.

"But Jack, I wasn't laughing at you; I was laughing at Max," said Bonkers. "Besides, I would never laugh at dreams—especially not at dreams about the Mothership."

Once again, Bonkers burst into uncontrollable laughter as Max zoomed past, this time standing on his front paws, his tail up in the air, crazy sparks shooting from its spiraling tip.

"You know, Bonkers," said Jack. "Sometimes you don't make any sense. First, you talk about the Dog Planet, as if you believe like a little pup. Then you laugh like a hyena at even the slightest mention of it."

"Jack, I'm sorry," said Bonkers, catching her breath. "It's just that Max is so funny. You really can't see him?"

"Oh, Bonkers, Bonkers," said Jack, shaking his head and then placing it down on his front paws. "I'm beginning to fear for the soundness of your mind."

Max shot past again, standing up on his front paws as before, except this time he was looking in the wrong direction, facing where he had been rather than where he was going. There was a huge crash and a blinding explosion of fireworks as he collided with a tree.

"Max! Max! Are you okay?" called Bonkers as she ran to help. But when she arrived, there was nothing to see. No Max, no skateboard, no scrapes on the tree; nothing out of the ordinary. Just sunshine and singing birds.

"Max?" she tenuously called. No answer.

"Bonkers, come here and lie down. You need some good morning sun," said Jack. Bonkers took a last good look around to make sure all was well before she joined him.

Both dogs lay on the pavement and turned their bellies to the warmth of the first basking sun of the season. It was a Saturday, and the people were still indoors, lingering in their beds, eating cereal in their sunny kitchens, or watching cartoons. There was no activity in the street, save for the occasional newly hatched bug spiraling past, or the tiny brown pieces of old leaves that had stubbornly remained through winter only now falling to earth after being pushed out by new growth.

"Jack," asked Bonkers, "You really don't believe *anything* about the dog planet? Not a thing?"

"Well," began Jack. "Let's see...all dogs dream of it. And they all seem to dream some of the same things; a huge spaceship-planet, lessons on how to be good dogs, different beautiful lands with everything a dog could want—that sort of thing. And they all seem to be left with the same feeling; of having a homeland, a place of belonging."

"Well...," surmised Bonkers, "if all dogs dream the same dream, then it must be true. Otherwise, how could *all* dogs have memories of the same thing?"

"You're mistaken, Bonkers," said Jack, shaking his head. "Those are not memories. They're just stories their parents have told them, as they were told by their own parents, and so on back in time. Fairy tales, told to pups."

Bonkers thought about how she had the same dreams, and she had no parents around to tell her any of those stories. *They have to be true,* she thought.

"You say the Dog Planet is just a fairy tale, Jack," said Bonkers. "But I don't believe that's all there is to it. I wonder what our other friends think—how about Bear, or Lula&Orbit. Or even Eddie—how about Eddie?"

"Are you addressing me?" asked the cat in perfect Doggle. She sauntered into the sunny spot and sat between the two dogs, twitching her tail. "I have never dreamed in all my days of a Dog Planet, or a Dog Ship, or anything of the sort. Therefore, since I *am* a dog, I can proclaim without equivocation that no such thing exists." She turned her face upward, looked down at Jack and Bonkers with a self-satisfied sideways glance, and flicked her tail.

The two dogs looked at each other with amusement. Although Eddie was an honorary dog, it was different from being an actual dog. For one thing, she didn't have the same desires, thoughts, or instincts. For another, she absolutely detested water, even when good fun depended on getting wet. Moreover, her feline traits often betrayed her wish to act and be seen as canine.

"Hey, Eddie. Why don't you ever *wag* your tail, like all the other dogs?" taunted Jack.

Eddie gave him a *look*, indicating the question did not merit a response. She curled her mouth with a bit of contempt, gave a decisive flick of her tail, turned with a flourish, and departed majestically with her nose held high.

The two dogs had a little laugh when Eddie was out of earshot, and then continued to bask in the sun. Bonkers let her thoughts wander. *Maybe Eddie doesn't have the same dreams because she's actually a cat, not a dog. Jack did have Dog Planet dreams, but he says he doesn't believe they are more than just dreams. I'll bet Eddie can't see Max just like Jack, but I can. Is it possible I'm the only one who can see Max, because I'm the only one who believes?*

At that moment Max flew by again, this time literally flying, as his teeth held tightly to the string of a kite that sailed high overhead. Bonkers once again laughed, and Jack groaned and turned over.

Bonkers watched until Max sailed out of sight and then lay her head down on the warm pavement. She thought about her life on the Dog Planet, her freedom, her education, her responsibilities as navigator, and her old pal Max. She thought of her life on Dirt, of her home, her boy, and her family. She thought about her friends, her neighborhood, and her Woods-in-the-Back. She turned all those thoughts inside out, upside down and backward in her mind.

"You know, Jack," said Bonkers, "life on the Dog Planet was pretty good."

"Yeah, yeah," he said, yawning with disinterest. "So I hear."

"You know what else? Life here on Dirt is pretty good, too."

Jack turned once again to face her and smiled. "Yeah, that it is, pal— and a doggone good world Dirt is."

VII. Adventure in the Big Forest

Bonkers and Jack were taken for a walk in the Nature Park by Curtis James and Livvy, the girl next door who belonged to Jack. Livvy had a little sister, Angela, who also belonged to Jack, but Angela was too small to keep pace with the others during a daylong hike. Consequently, it was Livvy alone who guided Jack on leash.

The Nature Park lay just at the end of the short cul-de-sac on which Curtis James lived, across a busy street. It was a big forest full of wildlife. In that forest, Curtis James had over the years encountered crafty raccoons and silent deer; spinning orb weavers, whirling water bugs, and globose slugs; tunneling moles and scampering mice; and birds of all sizes from great soaring hawks to small twittering songbirds. He had seen nesting ducks and bright-orange crawdads; scratchy-tickly centipedes and soft wooly bears; chittering squirrels and rat-a-tatting woodpeckers; shiny black beetles and buzzing insects; sun basking snakes and swooping bats; and countless varieties of creatures that live by the rules of nature. He had found all kinds of plant life as well, ranging in size from the tall coniferous trees towering overhead to flowers so tiny as to be almost invisible to the eye. The park also contained a nature center that educated inhabitants of the domestic world about their wild forest cousins, including some that Curtis James had never seen, such as small wildcats and coyotes.

Curtis James had visited the park many times previously, as had Livvy. Each time they went, they found something new and exciting. Today, the forest seemed to buzz with life as the children and dogs found their way along the path.

It was a sunny summer day; the very best of the season, very much like the day two summers ago when Curtis James had found his puppy underneath a fern frond. Now Bonkers was no longer that tiny pup, but had filled out into a fine dog. Her coat was thick and shiny, her teeth white and sharp, and her legs long and strong. She was a happy dog, and she walked with a proud chest and darting eyes.

Since Bonkers and Jack were on extendable leashes, they were able to trot ahead of the children. They were very excited by the unusual smells and noises. They constantly stuck their noses into and under things, ran ahead, wandered into the brush, ran sideways, tripped over each other, tracked backward before racing to the lead, and generally had a great time searching.

Not far into the woods, Jack stuck his nose into the air and stated, "I smell that invisible friend of yours."

Bonkers raised her nose to the breeze and caught the unmistakable scent of Max. The beagle had been no stranger over the past few months. He had made his home just outside of her window and was there every night when she went to sleep and every morning when she awoke. His foundation-rumbling, spark-zinging snoring often kept her awake at night, while all others in the house, incapable of hearing him, slept on. Max had taken to following Bonkers wherever she went, except for inside the house; Bonkers requested that he remain outside, since she was not at all fond of constantly being given baths.

The beagle had accompanied her several times on visits she made to her dog friends. All of the other dogs were able to smell his odor, but none had ever succeeded in actually seeing him. Bear might possibly have been an exception, but he never said a word about his being able to see Max, preferring as a general practice to keep such things to himself. By and large, most of the other dogs took to joking about Max and speaking of him in a teasing manner, referring to him as Bonkers' invisible friend.

Today in the woods, Bonkers looked around and saw, in the not-too-far distance, the now-familiar zinging, sparkling lights that accompanied the beagle.

"Hi, Max," she barked, and a distant familiar, "Do-ope!" was bayed in a response that only Bonkers heard. She was happy now. She was with Curtis James, her best human friend; Jack, her best dog-friend; and trailing nearby was Max, her best invisible-dog-friend. Together with her boy's good friend Livvy, they made something of an adventure team as they headed into the Big Forest.

Not too far into the woods, they reached a large blackberry patch where the children stopped for a sweet sun-warmed snack.

"Livvy," said Curtis James, "Do you think we'll find any treasure?"

"Do you mean the famous one, CJ?" asked Livvy. Livvy, short for Olivia, was the only person whom Curtis James allowed to address him by a nickname. Everyone else, even people in his own family, was compelled to use his entire first and middle names.

The famous treasure to which the children referred had a legend behind it: a long time ago, somewhere deep in the Big Forest, a stash of gold had been hidden. Many, many years in the past, long before anyone who was now living had been born, there had stood a huge mansion on the far side of what was now the Nature Park. One night, a sudden and fierce fire burned the mansion to the ground and killed everyone unfortunate enough to be trapped inside. Rumors spread that Master Hastings Grimshaw, the miserly and distrustful (and now deceased) proprietor of the estate, had some years before hidden a great hoard of gold coins in the forest, in a place only he knew about. Many people over the years had tried to find the treasure, but to no avail. Misfortune and death had befallen several of the treasure seekers: some had been thrown from spooked horses, some forever lost in the forest, and some stricken by strange, hideous diseases. Fantastic rumors spread and a legend was born. It was rumored that the site of the fire, now just the weed-overgrown remains of the foundation, was haunted, spooked by the spirit of old Grimshaw who was determined to protect his precious treasure from thieves and looters.

"Yeah, that's the one," said Curtis James, his voice betraying a hint of trepidation. He knew logically that ghosts and curses were not real, but he had a great imagination that forever beckoned to the wild and unbelievable.

"You know what? I don't believe in ghosts, and I bet if there really was a treasure, someone would have found it long ago." Livvy was always the practical one. Of the two friends, she was the one who kept a clear mind and looked at things with sensible logic. However, this in no way stopped her from looking at new things with excitement, nor from greeting fresh discoveries with awe and wonder.

"You know what else?" asked Livvy. "I bet we'll find treasures of the forest no one has ever found before. I bet we'll see things never even seen before. Come on—race you to the High Bridge!"

The two children ran downhill to the stream as fast as they could go, led by the excited dogs pulling on their leashes and urging them to go even faster. When they reached the bridge, Livvy and Curtis James lingered at the rail watching water bugs dancing in circles and leaves washing downstream. On the murky bottom, they spotted the bright orange glint of a fat crawdad just before it jetted backward under a rock.

The dogs pulled their leashes out as far as they would extend and sniffed around in the woods, Bonkers on one side of the bridge and Jack on the other. Jack turned over leaves and scratched in the dirt trying to find he-knew-not-what, and relishing the process of discovery. Bonkers, nose to the ground, peered into a thicket. As she raised her head, she saw sparkles and little flashing lights not more than a few steps away.

"Max!" she said.

"Who are you talking to?" called Jack from across the stream. "Oh, never mind," he said as he realized who it was, and continued his search in the underbrush. He had gotten used to Bonkers carrying on conversations with her imaginary friend while he just went about his business.

"Hi, Bonkers," said Max, playfully bounding and jumping. "Hey, come and looksee what I have." Out of his mouth, he placed several small objects on the ground in front of Bonkers.

"What are they?" she asked.

"These are my treasuries. I corralled them from all over, and each one is a rememberandum of something. Wanta see? Look at this." He nudged toward her a small piece of fern that appeared to have been pressed and dried. "This is from the firstest thing I saw on Dirt, from just right where you founded me. I went back that night and bit off a little-bit-piece, and then I asleeped on it every night until it was very-terrier flattened out and drieded up." The fern sparkled a little bit, just like Max.

"And looky—here are some prettiful beads;" he continued, nudging the pieces toward Bonkers as he described them, "and some prettiful rocks; and some furstalks—you know, the kind that grow out of birds; and a rubbery yellow ducky without a head; and a couple o' those shiny, round metal thingies humans like to carry in their pockets; and a birdie skull; and—oh, here's the bestest part—a rottening egg; and some rottening peaches; and all kinds of things that smell goodyyummy, like a rottening slug; a stink bug (I take care of him and feed him so he likens me); oh—and this great pinecone—smell it—I think it was sprayed by a skunk; and still-gooey dirty chewing gum; and some soggymoldy French fries...now where did they go? Oh, yeah, I ate them. Anyways, I memberize all the areaspots where I got them from, and what I was doing when I got them. It's my recollection of rememberies from Dirt."

Up on the bridge, Curtis James asked, "Do you smell something, Livvy?"

"Yeah, and it's pretty stinky," she replied, wrinkling her nose. Then she thought for a moment and said, "But that's okay; it's all part of nature."

"But Max, how do you fit all of them in your mouth?" asked Bonkers, looking at the large pile at her feet. "And how do you keep from slobbering all over them?"

"I don't know," said Max, looking puzzled. "Let me workthink on it." As had happened before, when Max pondered on something, strange thins began to occur. This time, his whole body began to glow brightly, and his ears stuck straight up in the air as if they had been pulled by wires. Then his head fell to the ground with a thud, and Max promptly disappeared with a 'poof!' and a shower of sparks.

Shortly he reappeared, lifting his head from the ground, and simply stated, "I just do."

Just then, Jack started to run around excitedly, sniffing loudly and pawing at the ground. Bonkers ran across the bridge to him and sniffed about. She discerned an odor she didn't recognize.

"What is it, Jack?" she asked.

"Something I don't smell too often." Sniff, sniff. "Something wild, as in not domesticated." Sniff, sniff, sniff. Jack's words became more excited after each sniff. "Something free and belonging to the outdoors." Sniff, sniff, whuffle, sniff. "Yes, I know exactly what it is." Jack lifted his head and peered into the trees. "It is the odor of coyote," he announced with assurance.

"Coyote," said a puzzled Bonkers. "What's that?" Without waiting for an answer, she took a long, studious sniff and said, "It smells of the wild as you say, but it also smells a bit like dog."

"That's what coyotes are," said Jack. "They're very much like us dogs, but they're not dogs. They're wild and live by their own rules, and they don't speak Doggle. They hunt for their food, and you have to be careful around them. If they are hungry enough they might take a young pup for their dinner."

"No, Jack! They would eat a dog? What kind of creature would do such a thing?" Bonkers had always lived a comfortable life, protected from the dangers of the wild world.

"I'm sorry to tell you, but it's true, Bonkers. Coyotes mostly eat rodents and big bugs, but one would eat a rabbit, or a cat, or even a puppy if it had to. It doesn't do it to be mean; it just doesn't have much of a choice, being wild and all. You have to understand—there is nobody around to just *give* food to a wild animal. If it didn't hunt for its dinner, it would starve to death. A wild animal isn't bad; it's just trying to stay alive. It's just the way the world works."

"Just the way the world works," repeated Bonkers pensively. "I don't think I like *every*thing about how the world works." Nevertheless, her thoughts rapidly lost their focus from the eating habits of coyotes as she became engrossed by thoughts of what it would actually be like to live as a wild animal. *What would it be like to run free,* she wondered, *and go wherever I want? Whenever I want? It would probably be pretty good, like in my dreams of the Dog Planet. What would it be like to live in a coyote family? To live by animal rules, with no commands from humans, no being told to sit, no leashes, no—*

"Come on, girl." Curtis James' voice interrupted her thoughts, and he gently tugged on her leash. "We have forest treasure to find!" Bonkers readily left her daydreams and ran to her boy.

Livvy called Jack, and the four adventurers ran up the path only a short way before they reached a fork in the road. Curtis James unfolded the trail map, and the children looked at it. Strangely, it didn't depict any fork in that particular spot. They thought over the situation carefully and decided that the path to the right looked intriguing; deer tracks wove through it, and it led to some distant tall trees. It seemed like a good trail from which to catch glimpses of the wild world, to find discovery and adventure. The children did not yet know it, but they had chosen a path that led off the map, a path that led into the deepest part of the forest, to somewhere near the ruins of the old Grimshaw estate.

As everyone waited for Curtis James to refold and stash the map, Bonkers took a moment to look behind. There she saw Max, his tail spinning whizwag, searching thoroughly in the area where Jack had found the coyote scent. His head suddenly shot up and he excitedly bayed, "Do-ope!" Nose and tail held high, he raced off in a shower of sparks, hot on the trail of coyote. Abruptly, with a thud and a flash, Max's sparkling trail was stopped short by the trunk of a tree. Shortly the sparkles reappeared and frantically veered around the tree, once again tearing through the woods, led by a fervent, "Dope…dope, dope!"

VIII. Coyote Gold

The adventure gang was now deep in the woods. They had hiked without rest for nearly an hour since the fork in the road, and the noises of civilization had long since become inaudible; there was no distant swoosh of cars, no voices of other hikers calling to each other, not even the drone of overhead airplanes. It was beautiful where they were, with glimmering streams and subtly hued flowers, and there were many blackberries to eat. The children traveled in excited circles from one blackberry treat to another until they had little sense of where they were in the forest. They did not worry, however, since the warm sun was high in the sky, and Curtis James had his compass in his pocket. They also knew they could rely on Jack's nose to find their way home if the need arose, and so they enjoyed their summer sojourn without care.

The dogs, however, caught the scent of something. Something approaching rapidly.

"Rain," said Jack, sniffing the air.

"Yes, I smell it, too," said Bonkers. She absolutely loathed getting wet, and she looked around nervously for shelter. The approaching storm with its distant rumble of thunder was now faintly audible to her, but not yet to the unsuspecting children.

"CJ—look! Over there," said Livvy. Ahead of them was what appeared to be the ruined foundation of what had most likely been a man-made structure. It was an area of level ground in the shape of a rectangle, with stones loosely piled along the perimeter. There were some scattered scrub bushes and some small trees obscuring part of the area, but the rectangle's outline was nonetheless discernible. The children started exploring in the center of the foundation and circled outward, until they found several more level areas that connected to the first with shared piles of stones. These stones had most likely formed walls long ago. The entire area was somewhat hidden by brush, but by poking around, the children soon made out what was the near-complete foundation of a large house. Behind an overgrown bush, central to the level areas, they found a sizeable stone formation that still partially stood.

"Look—a fireplace," said Livvy, gently kicking one of the smaller loose stones at the base. "It was huge. I guess it had to be in order to heat such a big house."

"Do you think it's part of the Grimshaw estate?" asked Curtis James, with just a hint of fear revealed in his voice.

"Maybe...I'm not sure. Say, where exactly are we, anyway?"

"Hmmm.... Well, I know we haven't ever been here before," said Curtis James, with more pensive thought than worry. He was nearly certain they couldn't be dangerously lost and was more curious than afraid. He knew the layout of the park well, but this uncharted territory was new to him. The trail that had led them to where they now were had been narrow and winding in parts, often resembling a deer trail more than a human trail, and the path had at times been vague and difficult to follow.

Suddenly, the sky darkened ominously. A slight flicker of lightning was closely followed by a blinding flash and a ground-shaking boom of thunder.

"Uh-oh," said both children together.

With a sudden ferocity, rain poured from the sky in buckets. The children and dogs ran blindly, trying to find some kind of shelter.

"Look—over there!" shouted Livvy. Not far ahead was a small cave, partially hidden behind some bushes and vines. They quickly pushed inside and huddled together. There was just enough room for all of them, children and dogs, but none to spare. They were all rather wet, but not completely soaked through, although Bonkers was wet well beyond her comfort level. The four friends stayed inside their shelter and watched the deluge fall in buckets from the sky to gather on the ground, forming turbulent claws of water digging into the forest floor. Lightning illuminated the midnight-murky forest with strobe flashes, and thunder pounded deep down to the roots of the tall trees.

"I wonder how long this will last," said Curtis James.

All of a sudden, just as quickly as it had started, the cloudburst ended. The rain eased ever so slightly and then suddenly stopped, and the sun shone as brightly as it had before. The rumbling thunder followed the disappearing clouds, and the sunlight revealed many glistening rivulets, made brown by dislodged mud, rushing down the forest hills. Steam rose all around and created a beautiful picture across the landscape, making it wet and misty, illuminated by soft, yet piercing sunlight. It seemed as if the sky had come down to earth: the steam formed into clouds that traveled across the forest, gliding silently through the trees.

The four tumbled out of the cave, the dogs shaking the water out of their fur and the children running their fingers through their hair to pull it out of their faces. The sun immediately warmed and started to dry them.

Bonkers stopped shaking and stood squarely still, looking puzzled. "Jack," she queried, "Do you smell anything?"

"Just the fine aroma of the fresh earth after a summer downpour," he replied, breathing in with deep satisfaction. "Why do you ask?"

"But you don't smell our trail, do you? The one that leads to home. I can't seem to pick up on it after the rain."

Jack sniffed the air, and searched the area, but to no avail. "You're right," he said. "But it's okay—your boy has his compass."

As if he had heard, Curtis James pulled his compass from his pocket. "Let's find out where we are." He tapped it once or twice, scratched his head, and turned to face a different direction. Then he looked up at the sun, tapped it again, and faced another direction. He did this a few times.

"What's the matter, CJ?" asked Livvy.

"I'm not sure. The compass doesn't seem to be fixing on a position. It keeps pointing in all different directions." He peered closely at the dial. "It's fogged, like it got some water in it."

"Oh, don't worry about it," said Livvy, thinking of all the people who hiked into the park every day. "We're bound to run across someone soon."

Bonkers, however, was troubled by thoughts of being lost in a forest inhabited by coyotes. She went over to Jack and nuzzled his ear. "Now what are we going to do?"

"We'll be okay," said Jack, bravely trying to sound nonchalant, knowing exactly what Bonkers was worried about. "I'll take care of us."

"But how?" asked Bonkers, a question for which Jack had no reply.

Time passed lazily in the forest. The sun, which had been high overhead, found its way lower in the sky, and the air became cooler. The kids and dogs found their way back to the ruins they had stumbled across just before the rain. Not extremely worried about the possibility of being lost, the children explored and made up stories about the people who had once lived there and about where the treasure, if it existed, had been hidden.

Curtis James and Livvy filled up on blackberries, but they were running low on their water, which they shared with their dogs. The children figured out which way north was by watching the progress of the sun, but that knowledge was of little help since they had wound around so many twisted trails to get where they were now. They simply did not know which direction led toward home. The nip of evening came into the air.

Suddenly everyone, child and dog alike, was greeted by a familiar and pervasive aroma carried on the breeze.

"I smell your friend," said Jack.

"Max!" exclaimed Bonkers.

"Hey, Livvy," asked Curtis James, "Do you smell that?"

"Yeah—it's that stink we smelled over by the High Bridge," said Livvy. "I'll bet if we can figure out where it's coming from, it'll lead us back to the creek." The children knew the way home from the High Bridge very well.

"Come on!" said both Curtis James and Livvy together. They didn't need to lead the dogs to the trail of the stench, since Bonkers and Jack were already pulling ahead, tracking Max's malodorous bouquet. They all ran swiftly through the forest, their chilled bones rapidly becoming warmed by the activity. Even better, they knew that each step brought them closer to the safety of home.

Of course, Bonkers was the only one who could see and hear Max, as the others were limited to perception of only his smell. Bonkers gave him a greeting of excited barks, which he returned with bays of, "Do-ope!" as he ran through the woods. Max led the way along the now-hidden trail the friends had followed on their way in. With sparks flying and tail spinning, he created a crazy wake of spiraling sparks trailing behind him. When Bonkers couldn't see the actual beagle, since he kept disappearing and reappearing in his excitement, she could follow his ensuing electric trail. Once or twice, she heard a thud and saw a zinging burst of sparkles at the base of a tree. Before she could ask Max if he was all right, the crazy path of sparks was once again tearing through the forest.

Bonkers and Jack raced hot on the trail of Max, tugging the gasping children along behind them. In no time at all, the adventurers were safely at the High Bridge.

"We did it!" shouted Livvy, as she and Curtis James panted to a halt on the bridge. The two children gave their dogs hearty pats and hugs as they stopped for a short while to catch their breath in the familiar surroundings. The lowering sun spread rays interspersed with long shadows, enveloping the world in warm golden hues. Birds twittered as they settled in before nightfall, and bats began to emerge for their early evening mosquito hunt. The smell of a not-too-distant evening barbeque wafted into the Big Forest. The engulfing stillness was only slightly interrupted by the far-off drone of a lawn mower.

"Hey—that stink we followed is gone," observed Livvy. Once again, they were surrounded by the fresh aromas of the water, the soil, and the trees. There was no hint of Max's putrid fragrance.

"You're right," said Curtis James. "That's strange…really strange. This is the spot where we first smelled it, isn't it?"

Lost in her own thoughts, Livvy didn't answer his question. She said, "I wonder what would have happened if we had not been able to follow it. Y'know, we should have been more careful. I bet it gets cold in these woods at night. I hear coyotes come out then."

Curtis James knew he was too big for coyotes to bother with, but he was still a bit scared. Mysterious beings, those he knew little about and especially those that came out in the dark, sometimes frightened him. Thinking about this, his mind wandered to thoughts about the ghost, and his spine shivered.

"Race you home!" he shouted, trying to sound brave, and he ran up the path, soon to be overtaken by the dogs and joined by Livvy.

That night before bed, Bonkers as usual went outside to meet with Max. The two friends customarily met every night, but tonight was different. It was special; Max had saved them from the deep forest, and Bonkers was bursting with questions.

"How did you know? How did you find the path?"

"I don't know how I knowed-it-all. I just did," answered Max. "And the path was easy to find. I just smelled it. Didn't you?"

"No, I didn't," replied Bonkers. "The trail was washed away by all the rain." She thought a minute. "Maybe the laws of the planet Dirt don't apply to you, since you are from the Dog Planet."

"Hmmm...it sounds fleasible," said Max. "Hey Bonkers—you know what I founded in the woods? Coyotes!"

"Coyotes?" Bonkers was all eyes and ears. "What were they like?"

"Curious making—so I watched them. They didn't seem to notice me though; just went about their stuff as if I wasn't there. There was a big male and a fleamale and a cub, and then another cub and then one more…and one more…and one more. They talked to each other, but I didn't know their words. I don't think they speak Doggle." Max started glowing. "Anyways, I followed them into their den. The cubs were having lots of fun, nipping and jumping on each other. I was only watching for a smidgit, when the two grownup coyotes put their noses up into the air and wrinkled up their faces, like they smelled something yuckypatootie. Then they pushed their cubs out of the den and they all ran away."

Bonkers imagined they had wrinkled up their noses because they thought Max's stink was coming from their den, and they had consequently run off in search of a cleaner home. She didn't think this would be easy to explain to Max. In the interest of hearing the rest of his story with expedience, she decided to say nothing about it at present.

"Anyways," he continued, "I explorated the forest for a while, and quick enough I ran into the big coyote again. He was alone this time. I stayed far away, becauseof…," Max looked a bit puzzled here, "well, just becauseof. Anyways, the coyote went far, far into the forest, pretty close to where I founded you guys. I saw him look around as if he wanted to make sure he was alone. Then he digged into the dirt. I couldn't see just what he was doing, but whatever it was, he did it for a while. Then he covered up the place he had just digged up with leaves and then ran away."

"What do you think he was doing?" asked Bonkers, listening intently.

"Well, I didn't know and I wanted to know and so I went to find out," said Max. "I went to the freshly digged-in dirt and digged it up myself so I could see. Do you know what I found? You'll never guess. They were prettiful—a whole big bunch of shiny round metal things the color of the sun. They felt cool and smooth, and they were flat and they had secret codes and pictures of human heads on them."

"Really? What do you think they were?"

"I don't know. But I borrowed one for my treasury collection. There were so many I figured a coyote wouldn't miss just one. Besides, coyotes probably can't count."

"Maybe *you* can't count," said Bonkers, "but I'll bet you those coyotes can count up to at least five." She was thinking of the number of cubs Max had seen.

"Maybe you're right," said Max, "but it was a zig-big bunch, and I took only just one. Come on close-up and have a look."

Max revealed his treasure collection, and smack in the center of it, overshadowing the others with its brilliance, gleamed the newest one. It was a round piece of gold, similar to the coins Curtis James had, except it was thicker and even more brilliant.

"Wow!" said Bonkers. "May I?" she asked, nuzzling it.

"But of corgis," answered Max, and she picked it up with her mouth. It felt heavy, heavier than anything else of that size that she had ever lifted.

"It's a real gold coin," she said. "I wonder if it's from the Grimshaw treasure."

"The whazzit?" asked Max.

"The Grimshaw treasure," repeated Bonkers. "It's rumored to be in the woods. Didn't you hear the kids talking about it today?"

Max just stood there, with a vacant look in his eyes.

At any opportune moment, Max's brain was given to drifting off into heavenly thoughts of food and becoming lost in them. Max had many opportune moments. Usually when he was not actually having a conversation, tracking a smell, or engaging in any sort of brain-taxing activity, Max was lost in gastronomical thought. Consequently, each time the children had discussed the treasure, he had not heard a word of the conversation. By the end of the day, he had accumulated a huge appetite but remained in blissful ignorance with regard to the legend of the treasure.

"Well, whatever it used to be, it's all coyote treasury now. Exceptin' for this one, of course," he said, looking closely at it. "I bet this'll buy a lot of beefy cookies when I get back to the Dog Planet."

"When you get back?" questioned Bonkers. "I didn't know you could leave here."

"Well, I'm not sure how," said Max. "but I know that somedaywhen I'll get back home. Feel it in my bones."

A whistle came from the house, the call for Bonkers to come in for the night. Max gathered up his treasures in his mouth, the dogs nuzzled each other goodnight, and Bonkers ran inside.

At bedtime, curled up on her pillow, Bonkers thought about her friend, the beagle savant. She thought about how he could not count to five and had flunked puppygarten repeatedly, and yet he was capable of tracking a trail even Jack could not. She thought of how he often clumsily ran into trees, and yet he was skilled enough to somehow hold all his treasures in his slobbery mouth without ruining them. She thought about how his mind simply became lost in thoughts of food instead of any useful contemplation, and yet he managed to find a treasure that for years had remained hidden from all other seekers.

She thought of these things until her mind became jumbled by the interspersed paths of too much thought, prompting it to simply shut down into quietness and allow her to drift into peaceful sleep.

As Max fell asleep, curled up under Bonkers' window, his uncluttered mind melted blissfully into musings about the warm marrow inside a stew bone steaming hot out of the pot.

IX. The Lure of Excitement

The bright morning light was clear and vibrant, causing Bonkers to blink her eyes before she trotted down the driveway. The leaves on the trees were large and dark green, with a slight hint of cadmium at the edges, and the brush underneath had turned brownish-yellow. The sun was still fat and golden, and the air was still warm.

Curtis James was in school once again, and consequently Bonkers set out early in the day to seek the company of the neighborhood dogs. She heard familiar yaps coming from across the street, and as had become her routine, she paid little attention and headed up the hill.

Lula&Orbit were out and about, tearing all around in great chaotic circles.

"Hi Bonkers!" yelled Orbit running past.

"Hi Bonkers!" yelled Lula running past in the other direction.

It looked like such fun that Bonkers jumped right into the game. After all, running in great chaotic circles was one of her specialties.

The three dogs ran as fast as they could, narrowly missing tree trunks and head-on collisions with each other. They made patterns, such as wild figure eights, and they played games, such as scaredy-cat. In order to play scaredy-cat, they ran at each other as fast as they could, and whoever veered out of the way first was the scaredy-cat.

During one particular game, all three dogs ended up running to the exact same spot. Realizing they were all about to crash, each tried to veer out of the way, but unfortunately each ended up heading smack into another dog. All three dogs collided with a huge BamCrunchThud, paws in the air, tails spinning, noses bent, and heads bonked.

"Bowser-OWser," said Lula. "I think I hear little birdies. We should know better than to play this game with a dog named Bonkers."

"Yeah," said Orbit. "Once again she lives up to her name."

"Hey! It wasn't all my fault," said Bonkers, sounding a bit upset. "We all did the same thing."

"We know, we're just teasing you," said Lula. "Just having a bit of fun. Fun is important. As a matter of fact, fun is the most important thing."

"The *most* important thing?" asked Bonkers. "Come on, aren't you exaggerating just a bit?"

"Nope, nuh-uh, noway. Not one little bit," stated Orbit firmly. "There is absolutely nothing more important than having fun. It is the only way to experience life to the fullest, to feel the blood rushing through your veins. Only if you have the proper amount of fun will you have a full life."

Orbit jumped into a nearby puddle and splashed Bonkers.

"Hey!" she yelled. Bonkers absolutely hated getting wet. "Why'd you do that? Now I won't be able to dry out for the rest of the day."

"Why dry out?" asked Lula, who jumped in the same puddle and splashed Orbit. "C'mon, Bonkers. Lighten up, pup. Sometimes getting wet is the best way to have fun."

"*Sharpei diem*. Make it your day, Bonkers. Enjoy life," said Orbit.

Lula&Orbit got into a splashing match with each other. There appeared to be no end to their fun. Bonkers just stood and watched as they played, feeling the uncomfortable dampness against her skin and the matting together of her fur.

When they tired of the puddle, Lula&Orbit ran downhill toward the trees. Bonkers took off after them, once again joining into the fun. The three raced through the trees, tore through the underbrush, and tumbled about in crazy abandon. Soon Bonkers became so engrossed in the games that she took little notice of small hazards and things that normally would bother her. As a result, she ended up becoming quite wet and muddy. However, unlike before, this time she paid little attention to her discomfort and thoroughly enjoyed herself.

The dogs played for hours, only stopping to take short rests in shady spots and to lap up drinks from flowerpots or occasional puddles. Near the end of the day, they were quite happy and also quite messy, scratched, and bruised. Bonkers had never before felt so elated and grungy at the same time. She was no longer bothered by the wet feeling, especially when there was so much fun involved. Neither was she bothered by the scratches and bumps with which she was now covered.

"Look! A car," yelled Lula. She got a frenzied look in her eye, shouted, "Whizwag!" and zoomed after it, Orbit hot on her heels.

Bonkers watched them go but didn't follow. She knew it was dangerous to chase cars. Scratches and bruises were one thing, but being run over by a car was final. She trotted down the street to home where she found Jack waiting for her on the front lawn. The two nuzzled noses and stretched out in a warm, sunny spot.

Over at Jack's house, no one noticed that the gate to Angela's play area had been left unlatched and ajar. No one saw when the small child set out from the safety of her home for the excitement of exploring a new area: the Woods-in-the-Back. Angela's parents were extremely busy dealing with a suddenly-leaking hot water heater and didn't notice much of anything except for the emergency at hand. They were busy sopping up the remaining water after the main had been turned off and rescuing what was salvageable.

"Dang! Look at this," moaned Angela's father as he held up some soaked photographs. "These are from our trip to the Grand Canyon."

"Don't worry about them," said Angela's mother. "We'll just rinse off the negatives and make new prints. Now hurry—come help me get the stuff from under this bed."

By the time Bear came by on his rounds and noticed the open gate, the child was nowhere to be seen. Bear bayed an alarm and all the neighborhood dogs immediately sprang into action. Jack put his excellent tracking ability to work and set off into the woods, followed closely by Bonkers and Bear. Eddie set off on some mysterious path of her own. Lula&Orbit split up and ran in opposite directions around the perimeter of woods. The little dog, Aldo remained yapping at the gate.

All the trails the dogs followed brought them to the edge of the woods, where they converged near a dangerous curve on the busy street. There they saw Angela, happily tottering toward traffic. They all stopped in their tracks, but only for a split hair of a moment, before they tore to the scene. Jack, with the help of Bonkers, went up to his child and tried to tug on her shirt in order to guide her away from the road.

"Yack!" she squealed happily as she reached for her pup. "Yack, buppy."

Bear stood in the road, solidly placing himself between Angela and danger. Lula&Orbit bravely ran out into traffic, darting in front of cars to divert them. There were loud squeals of tires and angry honks of horns as cars veered out of the way.

"Get outta the street you stupid mutts!" shouted one driver, shaking his fist. "You're going to kill someone—you're a menace!" Bear, knowing quite well he was neither stupid nor a mutt, stood his ground. Lula&Orbit continued to run into the road, where they were greeted by more squealing tires, honking horns, and angry words. Not one of the drivers saw the small child at the edge of the road.

Eddie walked up to Angela and gently rubbed against her and purred. "Kitky!" laughed the child and reached for Eddie. Before she could grab hold of the cat, Eddie took a step back, away from the street.

"Kitky! Here, kitky," said Angela, and she took a step toward the cat, and once again, as she was about to grab Eddie, the cat took a step away. Soon Eddie was leading the child back through the woods toward home and safety, followed by the dogs.

Back inside the waterlogged house, Angela's parents were suddenly greeted by a noxious odor.

"Oh, what now!" griped her mother.

"Ugch—that's horrible!" said her father. "It smells like a skunk or something." They both started choking and coughing.

"A skunk or something worse," gasped her mother. "Come on—we have to get outta here." They both ran for the door.

Eddie had just reached the play area and the dogs had just pushed the gate safely closed behind Angela when her parents frantically ran out of the house. Without noticing the dogs, they hurriedly picked up their child and unceremoniously shooed Eddie out of the yard. They jumped into the car and headed out to retrieve Livvy from softball practice and head out for a nice, relaxing restaurant dinner.

The dogs stood in silence for several minutes, facing the closed gate. "Well," said Jack eventually, "My family's safe." The other dogs nodded in agreement and one by one headed to their homes.

Bonkers noticed a lingering trail of sparkles that emerged from the house and vanished into the Woods-in-the-Back. She was the last to head home after bestowing her friendliest lick on Jack's nose.

She was given a bath as soon as she arrived home, even before she was given dinner. It wasn't so bad. MomSarah dried her with a soft towel and then used a warm blow dryer until she was all soft and fluffy. Afterward, she ate a satisfying dinner and lay at her boy's feet while he did his homework. Even motionless, she still felt the exhilaration and excitement of the day racing through her body.

The next day Bonkers went up the street in search of Lula&Orbit. She found them as usual, only this time things were different. Her two friends were tied up on chains, and there was something being built in their yard.

"Bonkers," said Lula. "Look what they're gonna do to us!"

"Lock us up in a jail—that's what. They said we were getting into too much trouble," said Orbit, putting on his best hangdog look. "Good little dogs like us, into trouble. Imagine!"

"All we were doing was having a little fun."

"Not to mention saving little human children from horrible fates."

"So we chased a few cars. So we rolled in some stinkpiles. Big barkin' deal. It's not like anybody got hurt."

"First they kick us out of the house— "

"They did that a few weeks ago. Said we were too much work for indoors."

"And now look at what they're building—a kennel!"

"Bonkers, we are going to have to live outdoors always—even in the cold and rain!"

"And we will always have to be locked up."

"Oh horrible tragedy, what are we ever going to do?"

Bonkers didn't know what they were going to do. She felt sorry for them. She guessed they were going to have to learn to live in a kennel, whether they liked it or not. Maybe it wouldn't be so bad. She had heard of dogs living in kennels and liking it; that it was safe and secure, and that nothing could come to hurt them. Maybe Lula&Orbit would get used to it; maybe they'd even have fun.

"I'll never get used to being in a kennel," said Orbit, rolling over and playing dead. "I can't take it."

Well, thought Bonkers, *I guess it will take a little time.*

"How are we ever going to have fun again?" asked Lula.

"Of course you'll have fun again," said Bonkers, trying to sound encouraging.

"But how?" asked Orbit. "Have you ever been locked up?"

Bonkers thought about it. She had been kept in the house or the car, waiting for her family to return, but never caged. "No, I guess I haven't," she said.

She looked at her sad friends. She looked at the chains holding them and at the ominous cage forming in the partial shade of a tall tree. Warming in the late summer sun were the sweet smelling wood chips that had been delivered for the floor of the new kennel. Rising up from the ground, board by board, were its sturdy walls. Already spanning the top were thick beams, upon which the roof would be laid. Nothing was going to stop that kennel from being built.

Bonkers remained with Lula&Orbit through the morning to keep them company and headed back home when her stomach rumbled for lunch. She ruminated over her recent adventures as she trotted down the hill. *Fun is good. Maybe dangerous sometimes,* she considered, remembering the near-tragic fate of the fun-seeking small child, *but I'm careful. I'm glad Lula&Orbit taught me how to thoroughly enjoy life. Yesterday, I got all wet and muddy, had a thorn in my paw, nettle scratches on my nose, and lumps on my head—and nothing hurt. Nothing bothered me. Fun made it all terrific.*

X. Moon Howl

Fall, winter, and spring had passed. They had been seasons of little incident as far as bad things were concerned, and of simple pleasures as far as good things were concerned. Curtis James was growing into a fine human. Bonkers was a mature dog now, but in no way had she slowed down. Jack had a few gray hairs, Eddie was getting curiously wider, Bear was taking more naps, Lula&Orbit were just as playful despite their confinement, and Max had not changed a bit.

Once again, warm weather had returned and a special night was approaching. It was the night of Moon Howl, the annual dog holiday, occurring on the first full moon of summer. On this night, all dogs did whatever was necessary in order to gather together and howl at the moon. If they could not manage to come together en masse, they did their best to get outdoors and join in the chorus. If they could not get outdoors, they did what they could to make themselves heard from indoors. It was imperative, it was essential; it was the obligation of each and every dog to participate.

This year, Bonkers was ready for Moon Howl. The previous year, she had been unable to get out of the house and had been constrained to howl indoors. Her singing had fallen on decidedly unappreciative human ears, and her participation had ultimately been reduced to quietly whimpering in the garage as she was forced to listen to the howls of other dogs through walls.

This year was going to be different. The windows were kept open because the short summer nights were warm, and Bonkers had been surreptitiously working on making an invisible-to-the-eye tear along the edge of a window screen. She would be able to easily wiggle out unnoticed, which was just what she did after all her people were asleep.

Like all dogs, Bonkers had, over the course of the year, been practicing her poetry as well as perfecting her melodious howl. She paused to look at the luminous moon that appeared to be very large since it had just cleared the horizon, and then trotted up the brightly lit street. Some distant songs—songs composed in times of loneliness, times of joy, times of anger, times of love; songs composed in bitter cold, in blistering sun, in crisp fall air, in sweet wet spring; howls from dogs across the land—began to drift through the night world.

Beef cookies, cheese cookies. How they warm my belly! I need bacon cookies, chicken cookies...

Outside it is cold. Outside it is wet. A pillow in front of the fire for me.

Eat meat, eat meat. Meat, meat, meat. Eat meat.

Bonkers heard a deep, resonant howl coming from straight ahead. She saw the huge silhouette of Bear, his great nose pointed toward the sky. Bonkers sat quietly beside him, careful to not interrupt.

Mud between my toes, raindrops on my nose, adding to my woes. Webnub,

howled Bear, his great voice reverberating through the hills.

He saw Bonkers and cleared his throat, as if he had been caught unawares in an embarrassing moment. "I am afraid you happened upon my recitation of a piece for which I have a nostalgic weakness. I apologize for subjecting your ears to such doggerel."

"What's doggerel?" asked Bonkers.

"Bad poetry," he replied.

"But, Bear," said Bonkers, with genuine surprise, "I rather liked it."

"I am indebted to your kindness, my gentle canine," he said. "Veritably, any howl is a praiseworthy diversion. Have you prepared a verse for the nocturnal festivities?"

Bonkers nodded, pushed out her chest, raised her nose to the sky, and howled:

Rain, you are like little darts. You pop my bubbles.

"Very nice," said Bear. "From where did you learn such prose?"

"It's something my boy once said," replied Bonkers.

More bays and howls wafted through the night air. There were all kinds: high pitched and excited, low and booming, gentle and melodious, sad and drawn-out. Some were energetic and joyful, some calm and bluesy. All were unique, all portraits of the dogs who howled.

Crunchy, slurpy, chewy, burpy. Eggs all cheesy, over easy.

Soap stinging my eyes. Water in my ears. Alas, my beautiful smell is gone. Why, I ask, why?

Sent me away—said she wanted a cat. What sense is there in that?

Bonkers and Bear sat and listened. They gazed at the moon, glowing bright and magical, occluding the stars with its brilliance.

"Bear," inquired Bonkers, "why do we sing to the moon?"

"Observe," said Bear. The moon shone radiantly, etching itself on the eyes. "The lunar satellite of Dirt is an iridescent orb in the celestial heavens. It reminds us of the Dog Planet, the place of our genesis. It is for our Motherland that we pine; it is our original home that we serenade."

Bonkers looked at it and thought of the world that was the Mothership. "Yes, it does remind me," she said, "but why do *all* dogs howl. You believe in the Dog Planet, and I believe in it, but not all dogs believe. So why do *all* dogs howl?"

"Because, my bon confidante, *all* dogs in their nucleus possess the same recollections," said Bear. "Some lay claim to their disbelief, but truth be told, the spectacle of the argentine moon evokes cherished memories of our homeland in every one of our canine souls. We cannot help but to serenade the resplendent orb."

Bear raised his nose and bayed to the moon:

Once I ran free in my homeland. An exceptional world, a distant planet—afar, parsecs beyond the cerulean. ...Alas, vanished, except in dreams.

As if in answer, a song came from across the hills:

Our own world. Run by dogs—ruled by dogs. Never a leash. We were a family; we were as one.

The songs brought a sad joy to Bonkers, sadness for the loss of her first home and joy in hearing the shared memories in song.

"Are you saying all dogs have memories of the Dog Planet?" she asked.

"Most certainly. Even if a dog questions the existence of it," said Bear. "It cannot be argued that the Dog Planet is, in some manner, known to all canines. It has become a place of legend, a place to visit in our dreams, and a source of wonder and imagination. It is a fount from which ideas and imaginings issue, from which conundrums surge."

"A what?"

"A dream factory."

A light breeze carried a howl from afar:

Oh Moon of Dirt, great glowing tennis ball in the sky— what worlds that may lie beyond are eclipsed by your brilliance.

"Bear," she inquired, "What is it that makes us all alike? What is it that makes dogs dogs?"

"Pardon for a moment," said Bear. Then he howled:

Swallowed my pride; secured said bone. Lo, the indignity of mendicancy.

"What's mendicancy?" asked Bonkers.

"Begging," answered Bear.

More songs drifted through the night sky:

Went behind the door. Saw the man in the white coat. Where are they now?

Alone. Left by myself, all alone in a crowd. The cold creeps through the floor of this dank kennel. Nose to tail with strangers. Will I ever go home?

I live for my master; I will do anything for her. She is my parallel universe—dog spelled backwards.

"Contribute to the chorus, Bonkers," said Bear. "Present to us a lyric." She howled:

My boy is like gravy on my kibble, the bounce in my ball.
The extra, the essential—the more, the less, the all.

"Now, where were we?" said Bear. "Ah yes, I remember. You are curious about the fundamental essence of the canine, or as you inquired: 'What it is that makes dogs dogs?' Of course, there are the obvious traits: a quartet of paws, a caudal appendage, barkability, the desire to chase diminutive creatures, etcetera. However, the fundamental unifying factor, our encompassing common bond, is the memory of the Code of the Canines. The Code commands all dogs to be kind and loyal. Each one of us learned it as part of our education and coming of age on the Dog Planet. We can detect the Code when we peer with insight into each other's eyes; we discern in the inner essence of each dog that same awareness and comprehension, that identical common bond from our homeland. Kindness and loyalty unite us into one."

"The Code of the Canines," contemplated Bonkers. "I always felt compelled to be loyal and kind—I just thought that was the way I was. I didn't realize it was something I had been taught."

"Most definitely. We were taught everything we needed to know to be virtuous canines here on Dirt. What humans consider in us to be merely instinctual or innate cannot begin to explain the scope of our knowledge and intellectual abilities. We studied industriously and learned countless duties and responsibilities before we arrived here. We are highly complex."

Aldo, the little yappy dog, wandered by just then, howling:

Owwwwwww, yip, yip, wowowwwwoooo...

"Of course," said Bear, "some are more complex than others."
More songs resonated through the night:

Seven! How could I have had seven? What am I, a cow? I need some sleep.

Burrs in fur, gnaw that paw. No matter—I have the biggest squeaky toy of all.

Stay, they say. Stay. Do they ever have to stay?

Bonkers felt compelled to add:

Wild and fast, free at last. Let go the leash—I must run!

Bear looked at Bonkers with a studious appreciation. "Bonkers," he said, "I perceive in you a fine quality of strength and vivacity. Indubitably, I observe a quality of invulnerability in your personality; your eyes are ignited with a fiery electricity of intense, torrid sapphire. Life is vibrant within you. It cannot elude you—you have captured its flame."

Bonkers, rendered mute by his complimentary statement, merely looked at Bear with intent curiosity. Racing through her mind were his words; words that jostled awake thoughts that had long been hibernating in crevices, that now filled her mind with questions and wonder.

The brilliant moon had passed the halfway mark on its journey through the night sky. "My young friend, the moment of my evening departure expeditiously approaches," said Bear. "Before I retire, I shall recite my alpha howl, the initial howl I learned as a pup: my concluding contribution to our annual canine cantata."

He rose to full height and bayed deeply and unhurriedly:

Warm dirt, inviting sun. Heaven.

"Perfect for the last sentiment of the evening," said Bonkers.

"Please remain—amuse yourself," said Bear. "I should favor listening to your splendid poetry as I drift into slumber."

"G'night, Bear," said Bonkers. After she watched her giant friend lumber inside, she sat and reflected on his words, her racing thoughts punctuated by the far off howls of dogs.

Chewed on a rock. Broke a tooth. Ow.

Bonkers thought about her inner vibrancy.

Took a drink from a puddle. Swallowed a worm. Stomach wiggles.

She reflected on the captured flame in her eyes.

Wind blows into my slap-flapping ears, echoes through my head, ricocheting, reverberating.

She ruminated over her pursuit of the intense fire of life.

Curse this chain that holds me! Freedom! Let the sound of it echo through the hills. We will revolute!

Bonkers began to become very tired. The moon was lowering in the sky. The world was calming, becoming still, darkening in the short hours before the sun was to rise. The howls of the dogs started to lessen and die out.

At last, my love, you have found me! I will forever share my blankie with you.

I have a home. I have food. I have a red rubber ball. Happiness.

Silence. Bonkers sat and listened to it. The moon had set. The world around was very dark, without a sound. Comforting. She felt free and safe.

Cast asunder. Torn away. Oh, how I miss my sandy beaches, my green hills, my prettiful Motherland.

Silence once again. It had been Max who sang the last poem of Moon Howl. Only he and Bonkers had heard it. All other dogs slept; some curled under the shining stars; some indoors on soft pillows; some in doghouses, the smell of night earth in their noses. Bonkers stood, stretched unhurriedly, and headed for home.

The languid silence was suddenly shattered by a far-off eerie sound coming from the forest. It started with crazy, laughing barks that transformed into long, high-pitched, wailing yowls. It was not a sound made by dogs. More chaotic barks followed more tremulous howls. It was a wild sound. The hairs on Bonkers' spine stood up and a shiver passed through to her bones. Coyotes! That's what they must be—coyote howls. The hysterical wails rang through the darkness, piercing the air with wild clarity.

Shaking with fear, Bonkers ran home like a streak of fire. The wailing seemed to follow her. Crazy laughing and yipping she heard, mysterious howls, penetrating to her core. She jumped at the window, pushed aside the broken screen, and scrambled into the house. She took cover under Curtis James' bed, and remained hidden there for many hours, until the wild cries had long since ceased and the sun was high overhead.

XI. A Rift and a Gift

Curtis James and JoelDad lazed in the tree house eating popcorn and drinking lemonade. It was a quiet, contented afternoon. Honeybees circled in the air, looking for bright, sweet smelling flowers. JoelDad had built the tree house when Curtis James was small, and over the years, the boy had made it into quite an extravagant fort. He used it as a spy headquarters, adding secret contraptions and espionage instruments. He also used it as a nature laboratory, studying caught bugs before releasing them, making experimental concoctions, and growing mold gardens. He built an extensive ant farm and observatory, with several living and viewing chambers connected by clear tubes through which he could see the ants crawl.

Curtis James took a break from his snack to fill the birdfeeder he had put high above the ground, just within reach from the tree house. JoelDad had a few last bites of popcorn that he washed down with a few last sips of lemonade.

"Time to get back to work," he said. He climbed down the ladder and continued his chore, which was clearing moss from steppingstones and pathways. He patted Bonkers, as she lay basking in the sun on the lawn, and then walked around to the other side of the house. Curtis James climbed down and took the cups and popcorn bowl inside to the kitchen sink.

He returned outside hitting a bright orange punching balloon. He punched it hard, and it made loud thwacks over and over as it hit against his fist. The balloon zoomed out and zoomed back even faster, making a bright orange blur in the sunlight.

The punching balloon frightened Bonkers. She didn't understand how something so big could be so light and travel through the air so fast. *It's not natural,* she thought. *And what exactly is it? Is it alive?* She watched it closely as it flung itself back at her boy each time after he hit it away. *Holy chow! It's trying to attack my boy,* she thought. *He's just punching it away in self-defense, trying to keep it from hurting him.*

"Hey—Pumpkinhead!" shouted Bonkers at the balloon, "You leave my boy alone! Stay away or you're gonna be sorry—back off!"

Thinking Bonkers wanted to play, Curtis James laughed and punched the balloon toward her. Since he had no understanding of Doggle, the boy had misinterpreted her anger toward it as playful barking. He attributed the wild look in her eyes and frenzied pitch in her bark to the fun she was having going after the crazy orange toy.

When it flew at her, Bonkers thought the balloon, incited by her threatening words, was trying to attack her as well as Curtis James. She was certainly not going to be bullied by any old floaty ball-thingy! She couldn't imagine why it would want to hurt her boy, but as sure as she had four paws, she was not going to let it.

"I said back off!" She lowered to the ground menacingly. "You're askin' for it!" Her eyes almost popped out of their sockets and her frantic yips seemed to originate from her tail and grow in strength as they passed through to her mouth.

Curtis James laughed himself silly, rolling in the grass. "Bonkers, you are the most fun dog anyone could ever have."

While he was down on the ground, Bonkers tried to lunge at the balloon. The boy kept pulling it just out of her reach, which was rather easy for him to do, since he was by far the calmer of the two. Bonkers had to wind up in a frenzy before each attack, allowing Curtis James plenty of time to pull the balloon out of the way.

After a while, the boy tired of the game and climbed the ladder to put the punching balloon on the tree house floor. "We'll leave it up there for later, girl. Now's time to get to work." He patted her on the head.

He picked up a yard bag and went off in search of weeds. JoelDad paid him a penny for each weed. It didn't seem like much, but it was a large yard and Curtis James was a quick weed picker. It didn't take him long to earn a few dollars. Funds were always low now when the days were long and he had time on his hands, and now was precisely when he needed those funds. He was saving up for a Mutant Turbo Blasterbot, the last model he needed to complete his collection of Blasterbots.

Bonkers sat in the grass and kept an unblinking eye on the punching balloon to make sure it didn't get any funny ideas. The balloon sat completely still on its perch in the tree house, but she didn't trust it. She suspected it was just waiting for the right moment to zoom through the air and attack an unsuspecting boy or pup.

Meanwhile, Curtis James pulled weeds near the patio where MomSarah was painting a chair. She often painted furniture when the weather was nice. She always said if it was the right size and the right shape, the wrong color was not a problem since that could easily be changed. The house was full of the more successfully changed pieces, and the patio became home to the less inspired ones.

All of the humans were busy with their tasks, their attention consumed. They didn't notice when a slight breeze nudged the bright orange punching balloon off its safe perch in the tree house. They didn't notice when Bonkers pounced on it and attacked, biting it angrily and shaking it furiously from side to side. They never heard the loud 'pop!' due to its being covered up by the drone of a low flying airplane. They never even noticed as Bonkers sat chewing it up until it was completely ruined, made irreparable by many tooth holes.

Soon the balloon lay motionless. Bonkers nudged it with her nose and waited. It didn't move. She growled at it and observed. Completely still. When she was fully satisfied the balloon could never try to hurt her boy again, she felt very proud of herself. She puffed up her chest and held her head high as she picked up the limp balloon to present to Curtis James.

The boy was busy at his work as Bonkers dropped it at his feet. At first, he didn't notice her gift. Bonkers took a short jump back and pointed at the balloon with her nose. Still her boy took no notice; certainly he would have kind words and pats for her—maybe even a bone. She went up to him and nudged him.

Curtis James turned and said, "What's up, girl?"

The instant he saw his ruined toy, his face fell and he blurted out, "Bad dog!"

Bonkers felt the world fall out from underneath her paws, taking her wounded heart with it. Curtis James had never spoken so harshly to her before. The words pierced like long needles, far into her center. She did not understand. How could she be bad, after she had so bravely saved him? She would do anything for him. What had she done that was wrong?

There was anger in his face, and it was directed at Bonkers. His tone had been harsh. She didn't understand why. She skulked off into the Woods-in-the-Back, her tail between her legs.

"What's the matter, hon?" asked MomSarah.

"Look, Mom. Look at what Bonkers did to my punching balloon," said Curtis James sadly. He held up the slobbery tatters to show her.

"Now why would she do that?" puzzled his mother. She thought about how the boy and dog had been playing with it, both seeming to have fun. She studied the chewed-up balloon.

"You know, I don't know why she did it," said MomSarah, "but she did bring it to you afterward. Dogs bring things to you when they think of them as presents. She probably thought she did something good."

Curtis James thought about that. *She did come up to me and present it to me like a gift. But why was she proud of destroying my toy, especially after we had so much fun with it?*

"Mom," he said. "Now I feel even sadder. My punching balloon is ruined and I don't understand why. But even worse—much worse—now Bonkers is gone." He peered into the woods where she had disappeared.

His mother gave him a hug. "She'll be back. All dogs come back at dinnertime. And you can always get another punching balloon."

"I don't care about any old lousy balloon," he said, tossing it into the garbage. "I want Bonkers back. She's my best friend."

But Bonkers did not come back at dinnertime. She was too ashamed. After a few hours, JoelDad left her food on the back patio, and Bonkers sneaked up in the dark to eat by herself. JoelDad peeked out the window and saw her eating. He didn't disturb her; he was confident she would come back to her family when she was ready.

Curtis James lay awake in his bed staring at the patterns on the ceiling for most of the night. He was worried that his dog had run away because of him, because he had frightened Bonkers too much with his yelling. The bedroom was lonely without her. His racing mind kept him awake with its worries and thoughts. *Was Bonkers afraid of the balloon? If so, was she trying to protect me? Then she must have been proud, only to have me yell at her.* It was horrible to think his best friend had run off because she was afraid of him.

After eating her dinner, Bonkers returned to the Woods-in-the-Back and thought things over. *How can I make things better? Maybe the balloon wasn't attacking Curtis James. Maybe it was some kind of strange human game, like fetch without the running. He certainly was sad when he saw it was ruined. I'd like to give it back to him, but how? If I could, I know he'd surely like me again.* It was horrible to think her best friend hated her.

"Hi, old pal." It was Max.

"Max, am I glad to see you," said Bonkers, jumping up and running to him. "I need a friend. I need help." She explained how she came to be in her troubled situation.

"I think I have the thingy you're look-searching for," said Max. He pulled the tattered orange punching balloon out of his stash of treasures. Now it was more than chewed-up; now it was also stinky.

"Oh, Max, you have it!" Bonkers did a flip, but she quickly lost her joy as she observed its condition. "But look at it. How can I ever fix it?"

"Let me contemplatter," said Max. As before when he called on his beagle savant brain for help, his ears stood straight up in the air and his eyes bugged out. However, this time he did not just glow and disappear. This time he stood stiff-legged and shot straight up in the air like a rocket, with jets of sparks shooting out of his four paws. Bonkers watched as he blasted up into the sky and then fell back to Dirt with a thud on the compost pile.

"Are you all right, Max?" she said with concern.

"Sure I am. Hey—it smells pretty goodelicious here." He rolled around a bit for good measure, but it wasn't long before he renoticed Bonkers' sad face.

"Sorry, pal," said Max, standing and shaking himself off. "I got canaried away. But don't worry—I thunk up how we can refix things. It's pure simplistication." He pulled a slobbery, chewed-on roll of tape from his treasures.

"Good idea," said Bonkers. "Let's get to work."

The two worked hard throughout the night. It was difficult for them to manipulate the tape, since they had no opposable thumbs and their best cutting instruments were covered with slobber. It took a long time, but by dawn all the holes in the punching balloon were covered by bits of tape. It wasn't pretty. There was dirt stuck to the tape in some places and slobber covering the adhesive in others, but overall, it was fine work for two dogs.

"Do you think it will work again?" asked Bonkers, examining it with hopeful optimism. "More importantly, do you think he'll like it?"

"One way to find out," said Max.

Bonkers picked up the repaired balloon in her mouth, carefully so as not to disturb or dislodge any tape, and walked quickly but with heed toward the house.

A warm ray of early morning sunlight streamed across Curtis James' bed where he lay finally asleep, exhausted and fitful, but asleep. His arm stretched across the bed, allowing his hand to fall over the side. Bonkers gently nudged his hand, her warm breath and whiskers tickling his fingers.

Curtis James awoke. There stood Bonkers, her eyes large and sad, with the taped-up punching balloon in her mouth.

"Bonkers!" yelled Curtis James, waking everyone in the house. He jumped out of bed and gave her a big hug. "I'm so glad you're back! I missed you terribly. I'm sorry I yelled at you." Bonkers dropped the balloon and licked his face.

JoelDad came into the room rubbing his eyes. "Look who's back," he said. "Welcome, girl."

A bleary MomSarah entered, tying her bathrobe. "Bonkers! Welcome home. I knew you'd come back."

As they all gave her pats, Curtis James remembered the punching balloon. He picked it up, examined it, and laughed with appreciation over what his dog had done for him.

"Mom, Dad. Look what Bonkers did! She fixed it," He lifted it up to show them.

"Bonkers did that?"

"But how could she? She doesn't have fingers."

"Amazing! How did she know what tape is used for?"

"What a smart dog!"

"What a good dog!"

Everyone surrounded Bonkers with pats and more pats. She was glad to be home, glad to be so warmly welcomed back into her family. She felt secure and safe again.

"What is that awful stink?" asked MomSarah. She took a good whiff of the repaired balloon. "Oh, I see. ...Well, I think I have of a solution. I'll frame it inside a shadow box and seal it very tightly so the smell can't escape."

"Yeah Mom," said Curtis James. "And I want to decorate the frame. With paint."

That is just what they did. When they were done, both the balloon and the red frame were beautiful. JoelDad hung the frame on the wall above Bonkers' food dish and made a small plaque to hang underneath that said:

Perforation Reparation
by Bonkers

Bonkers could not read the human symbols, but she sensed the plaque said something important about her.

Her family never did figure out how a dog could have fixed a balloon with tape, not even a dog as smart as Bonkers. They thought she had a special talent, and for many years, they proudly showed off the framed balloon to visitors. Curtis James did his best never to yell at Bonkers again, unless it was *absolutely* necessary, such as if she nearly ran in front of a car. Even then, he used a kinder tone. He never got another punching balloon; he did not want to frighten Bonkers, and more importantly, a better balloon than the one hanging above the dog dish could not possibly exist.

XII. To Be Smart and Kind

That evening, Bonkers went out for her usual visit with Max. Surprisingly, his normally pungent aroma seemed weak and distant. She saw some sparkles, but they were far off in the woods, past many trees and over hills. It was a late summer evening, and the sun was setting slowly and warmly.

Bonkers' nose detected a curious nearby smell—it was different from the norm, unusual for the backyard. She took a deep sniff and discerned the co-mingled aromas of sweet punch, chocolate, and Livvy. Bonkers searched for the source of the smell in the backyard and found that it came from up in her boy's tree house. As she neared the ladder, Bonkers heard sniffling. She looked up to see Livvy, dressed in a beautiful taffeta dress, with her feet clad in shiny black party shoes dangling over the edge. Bonkers saw that her cheeks were stained with tears. Dogs don't understand tears completely, since they themselves never cry with them, but Bonkers had seen them before and knew they came when a person was somehow hurt. Livvy saw the dog, climbed down the ladder, sat on a low rung, and buried her face in Bonkers' fur.

"Hi, Bonkers," she said, sniffling interrupting her words. "I was hiding up there for a bit" Sniff. "Just want to be alone" Sniff. "But you're okay. Dogs aren't like people."

Bonkers licked her hand. Livvy smiled a little, but just a little.

"Why are people so mean sometimes? Dogs aren't like that." Sniff, sniff. Livvy's thoughts were racing in angry and hurt circles through her mind. "I wish I had good manners. I wish I could know what to do. Then people wouldn't laugh at me." Bonkers rested her head in Livvy's taffeta lap and Livvy patted her gently. Bonkers did not exactly know what manners were. They apparently had something to do with knowing what to do. Could they be like the Code of the Canines?

"It was my cousins," Livvy said angrily. "They laughed at me when I didn't know which was the right fork. And when I put my elbows on the table. And when I licked my fingers. And when I did things wrong I still can't figure out. They laughed over and over. They even pointed their fingers at me." Angry tears pushed their way out of her eyes. Bonkers thought Livvy's cousins didn't sound very nice. She got mad at them for making her friend feel so sad.

"Even Angela pointed at me and laughed. My own little sister!" she cried. She calmed a bit and said, "Of course, she's too little to understand. She was just copying them." Sniffle. "I just wanted to have fun at my Uncle's wedding. I just wanted to wear a real pretty dress, eat cake, see everybody, and dance...only I never did dance. I figured if I had such poor table manners—well, just imagine how I would look on the dance floor." Bonkers imagined Livvy would look simply splendid on the dance floor. She licked Livvy's cheek and the girl smiled a bit.

"Oh, Bonkers, if only I had decent manners, no one would laugh at me." Livvy put her chin in her palms and kicked at the dusty earth, scuffing her party shoes a bit.

As Bonkers listened to Livvy, she got some idea of what human manners were. She guessed they had something to do with showing off that you knew more than someone else did, and then making that person feel bad. She didn't think she liked manners. She liked the Code of the Canines, which simply stated that in such a situation a dog should be kind. That was it. A dog should think of others and make them feel welcome with kindness. All that human stuff about forks and elbows sounded like complete nonsense to Bonkers. She decided Livvy needed to stop wasting her time thinking about it.

Bonkers spied an old, dirty tennis ball not too far away—the perfect diversion. She sprang up and retrieved it, making it decently slobbery before depositing it into Livvy's lap.

"Bonkers! My dress!" shouted Livvy, springing to her feet and flinging the ball off her. The sadness and anger on her face were for a moment directed at Bonkers. However, as Livvy saw the kind, playful dog face, her anger quickly turned to surprise. She thought. She thought about her cousins and how mean they were to her, and how much worse that was than not knowing table manners. She thought about this dog, indecorously ruining her dress. She thought about how Bonkers was only acting out of kindness. She thought about all these things very quickly. Then she laughed. She laughed and laughed. She kicked off her party shoes and hugged Bonkers.

"Bonkers, you are the sweetest, kindest dog there is!"

She picked up the ball, threw it, and raced Bonkers across the grass for it in her bare feet. The warm evening air had turned to cool night air, and the grass was soft and dewy between toes, beneath paws.

XIII. Loss

The earth was warm and sweet, as was the grass. The sun seemed to dissolve any of the wispy, lazily passing clouds that dared pass in front of it. Children jumped through sprinklers and splashed in backyard pools. Swallows swooped across fields in daredevil maneuvers, and squirrels jumped across the highest treetops just for the sport of it. Life hummed through the world. It came from everything and passed through everything. It sprung as a nasturtium from the soil; entered the air on the wings of a ladybug; landed on a child's finger and rode running through a field; rose high into the air on a kite; and eventually landed on a cloud, upon which it would stay until a raindrop brought it back into the soil.

As Bonkers trotted up the street, she sensed this life around her and inside her, feeling its buzz in the air and in her veins. As was her daily custom, she was heading out to meet with her dog friends. She expected to find them outside, either sleeping in sunshine or rolling in the agreeably warm, dry dirt.

She passed Jack's house without catching sight of him. That was not unusual, however; Jack was often roaming or visiting friends. *It's kind of quiet,* she thought and realized that the little yappy dog, Aldo, had not made an appearance. Neither had Eddie, but of course she never found Eddie; Eddie found her. She walked up past an oddly quiet Lula&Orbit's kennel (maybe they were still asleep inside their doghouse), and walked toward Bear's house. No Bear either. Now that was odd. Bear always occupied the street in front of his house from the moment the sun came up.

"Bear!" called Bonkers. No Bear.

"Bear!" she called again, louder. Still no Bear.

"Bonkers," called Jack's quiet voice from around the corner of Bear's home. There was something odd in the tone of his voice, something foreboding. Without knowing exactly why, Bonkers was afraid to approach. Despite her fear, she was strangely and inevitably drawn around that corner. As she went there, she had a feeling she was sinking, deeper and deeper with every pawstep.

Jack was waiting for her at the corner of Bear's house. She stood next to him and saw what lay ahead; all the neighborhood dogs except Bear stood in a circle, gathered around a fresh mound of dirt with a newly planted dogwood tree in the center. They were quiet, somber.

"Oh, Jack," said Bonkers. "No." The sinking feeling was abruptly replaced by the sudden sensation of the ground sliding away from under her.

"I'm sorry, kid," said Jack. "Bear was a good friend." He walked with her to the circle of friends around the grave. Each shaky step she took was accompanied by an awful, floating feeling. It was as if the world were not quite real, as if this were not actually happening.

"He had a full, happy life. Rich with experience." It was Orbit's voice. Bonkers half wondered how the two had gotten out of the kennel, but in the light of things, she quickly forgot. She saw some sparkles shooting up from behind some bushes and felt comforted to know Max was nearby.

"He was the best of dogs," said Lula. "So large and yet so gentle."

"He was my friend," stammered Bonkers. "We talked about... about...everything."

"He was like a father to us all," said Eddie.

"Yes, he was," said Jack, with sincerity. "He was our protector. He was also our teacher."

"Yes," said Bonkers. "He taught me about life." She thought about how life had now left him. What had become of him? She wanted to ask him, but he was gone. Just gone, leaving nothing but a terrible hole inside of her.

The dogs mourned for their friend quietly, comforting each other with kind words. They surrounded the new grave with somber dignity. Aldo, normally yappy but now silent, carefully placed a small bone atop the mound of earth and returned to his place in the circle.

As the dogs said goodbye to their friend, the world went about its business. The sun climbed in the sky, birds sang their songs, children laughed in the distance, a lawnmower buzzed, and bees busily hurried among the flowers. Bonkers took only remote notice of the continuing bustle of life in the world, illusively telling herself the activity was mere background music, setting the stage for a beautiful morning as an accompaniment to a warmhearted and conclusive farewell to Bear.

The sun climbed higher, and in turn, the dogs left for their respective homes. Jack and Bonkers walked down the street together.

"Jack," asked Bonkers, "why does it hurt so much?"

"It just does," he replied, shaking his head. "It just does." Jack remembered a long time ago, before he lived with his current family, when he had resided in the pound. He thought of the dogs who had not been lucky enough to find homes, and how he had missed them after they had been led from their cages for the last time.

"I feel so empty—like there is a part of me missing. Does it get better?" asked Bonkers.

"Yeah, sure it does. With time. A little better every day. But it takes a long time." He saw her hurt face and discerned on it the same hurt he himself felt inside. "It helps if you remember. If you make a place in your heart for memories of him, you can go there whenever you want to visit."

Jack nuzzled Bonkers' nose and headed across the lawn to his home. The sun, now high overhead, warmed Bonkers' dark fur as she continued walking slowly by herself. *With time.* She repeated Jack's words in her head. *A place in my heart.*

Soon after the sun had set and the shadows were busy chasing away any lingering light, Bonkers met Max in the backyard.

"Bonkers, I am very sympasorry about your friend," said Max. "He was a good dog. I know. I used to visit him sometimes. He would call out, 'Greetings, Bonkers' imaginary friend!' Then he would laugh. I'm not exactly sure how he knew I was there, when the others didn't," reflected the stinky beagle with bewilderment. "At any rate, he talked to me. I got all alonely sometimes, being invisible and all, but he could make it a-okay."

"Thank you, Max. I miss him."

"Yes, I do too." Max let his head sink, and something fell out of the corner of his mouth and hit the ground with a clink.

"What's that?" asked Bonkers, catching a glimpse of it. It appeared to be a pin, the sort of which would be used to lock a kennel.

"Oh, nothing," said Max, quickly picking it up and concealing it once again in his mouth. "Just a new treasury. A shiny thingy—no big deal."

"Max?" asked Bonkers, changing the subject, "What happens when we die?"

"I don't know, old pal," He paused for a moment. "I just have rememberies of the past. The future is all a coming mysteriousness. A wonderful mysteriousness." He sparkled and rapidly started to become transparent.

"Wonderful?" asked Bonkers. She certainly didn't feel wonderful now, and now was yesterday's future. Max did not answer, since he had already disappeared for the night. Bonkers sighed and trudged heavy-pawed inside to Curtis James' room. She was sad and exhausted.

When Curtis James saw her, he patted the bed, inviting her up to sleep atop the mattress with him. He knew Bonkers was upset over the loss of her friend; he himself had been very fond of the huge friendly dog. He wondered what he would do if Bonkers ever died. He became sad over those depressing thoughts, and tears fell down his cheeks. Bonkers licked them away, and soon the boy fell asleep. Bonkers, conversely, lay awake much of the night. She was kept so by a terrible emptiness inside, even though she lay curled up next to her boy.

XIV. New Life

Time passes very slowly when the heart is heavy and sleep does not come easily. The following weeks were rather uneventful, giving Bonkers further opportunity to dwell upon on her sadness. She thought about Bear and tried to fixate on good memories, but when she was by herself, this only made her feel more alone. It helped to go outside and visit her dog friends, all of whom had been Bear's friends. They wanted to talk about him, and their fond recollections seemed to bring him back, if only for a moment. She didn't feel so alone when she was with them, sharing their memories.

One quiet afternoon, during what was siesta time for most dogs, Bonkers visited Lula&Orbit. The pair had adapted well to the kennel, quite to the contrary of what they had expected. Certainly their world was smaller, but it was far from less fun, and now it was also safe and secure. The two dogs still constantly played the same games, the only difference now being that their play had to be modified due to spatial limitation. The source of their amusement had proved to come from deep inside of them;

no bars could come close to stopping or even remotely containing the amount of their fun necessitating release.

"Hey, Bonkers," said Lula, "have you seen Eddie lately? She hasn't been around for days."

All three dogs looked around, expecting Eddie to appear, as was her usual custom when her name had been mentioned. They waited for her to pop out from behind a bush or saunter around the corner of the kennel. Eddie, however, did not appear. *Odd,* thought Bonkers. *Highly unusual.*

"I wonder where she could be," said Bonkers with some concern. She recalled that the last time she had seen Eddie, the cat had appeared very tired and run-down. She also had looked a bit overweight, which was odd for the normally active feline.

"Eddie!" called Lula. "Eddie, where are you?" No sign of Eddie.

"Maybe we should form a search party," said Orbit. "Maybe she is in some kind of trouble and needs our help."

"Search party?" questioned Bonkers, looking at the bars. "But how? You two are locked up."

"Oh…," answered Lula evasively, "we have ways." Orbit nipped her on the ear, and she chased after him, tearing around the kennel, bark dust flying.

Bonkers looked perplexedly at the locked door and shook her head. She decided whatever it was that the two did to escape probably took a good deal of time. If Eddie was in danger, time was something not to be wasted.

"I'm going on ahead," said Bonkers, thinking of Eddie possibly trapped someplace cold and dark without food or water, or maybe even injured and unable to get help. She had to get to Eddie's house in a hurry— maybe the cat wouldn't be there, but at least it was a good starting point for her search. Maybe there would be clues. "I'll see you guys later."

She ran down the street, to Eddie's front yard and found…nothing. She went to her back yard and found…nothing. She walked up near the house, trying to peek inside the windows a bit (dogs don't find this to be bad manners) and saw…nothing. Absolutely nothing. She rounded the corner near the garage and heard a tiny little sound.

"Myee." Bonkers stood completely still, waiting to hear more.

"Mmmyee." There it was again. It sounded soft and sweet, very much like a baby bird.

"Myee…myee, mmmyyee." There were many of those little sounds, all coming from inside the garage. Bonkers nudged the door aside and went in. There was Eddie, looking tired but very proud, lying in the middle of five tiny balls of fluffy, soft fur. One was striped orange, two were black and white, one was just plain white, and one was brown, black, and white. They were very tiny, just the right size to cuddle in a human hand, and their eyes were still closed. They were all wobbly, wrinkled, and matted in spots, and their faces were scrunched up.

"Oh, Eddie," exclaimed Bonkers, "how beautiful they are!"

"Thank you, kindly," said Eddie. "They arrived very late last night, all healthy, and not one is smaller than the others. I'm very proud. I think I'll like being the mother of such fine pups." She smiled and licked a kitten that was soon lulled to sleep by its mothers' gentleness. She lifted the tiny creature by the neck and put it in a warm spot next to her fur. She replaced the first kitten with another, now giving this one a gentle bath until it too slept. She repeated the ritual until all of her children were asleep, after which point she lay down her own head.

"Eddie, I have to tell our friends," said Bonkers, trying to be quiet so as not to disturb the new family, but unable to keep her excitement from raising her voice a bit.

"Of course," said Eddie smiling proudly and sleepily.

Bonkers slipped outside. The bright sun caused her to stop for just a moment to blink in its glare, before she ran across the street, fast as a firework, her ears flying in the wind.

"Ja-a-a-ack!" she hollered. "Jack, where are you? Jack, come quick— Eddie had kittens!"

Three replies came from three different voices:

"Kittens!"

"Hot diggety dog!"

"Bowie-wowie! Let's go see."

Standing before her were not only Jack, but also Lula&Orbit.

"Lula? Orbit?" asked Bonkers. "How did you get out?"

"Never mind that now," said Orbit, getting a head start across the street. "C'mon, let's go see those kittens."

"They're beautiful," said Bonkers to her friends as they ran to the garage. "There are five of them." Pant, pant. "And they are adorable and soft. Even though they are baby kits—," pant, "they make sounds very much like those of little birds." Pant, pant. "Very sweet and tiny and high pitched."

As the four friends approached Eddie's garage, they quieted down and tiptoed up to the door. They cautiously poked their heads in the door, one on top of the other. When Eddie looked up, she was greeted by a shaft of light illuminating a totem pole of heads: Jack on the bottom, then Lula on top of him, then Bonkers, and Orbit at the very top. The little dog, Aldo, made his appearance, squeezing his head in at the very bottom.

Eddie laughed at the spectacle then said, "Come on in. Come see my new family."

The dogs tumbled through the door, regathered themselves, and then stood speechless and amazed at the sight. There was Eddie, rough and tumble Eddie, one of the gang Eddie, now incredibly transformed into a mother. There she lay in the middle of her new kittens, now so caring and gentle, revealing a side of her that had previously been hidden from her friends.

Even more amazing than the changes in Eddie, were the kittens themselves—how perfect and tiny and alive they were. The cat's children inspired great admiration from the onlookers, who watched quietly, so as not to intrude upon the new family. The observing dogs stood transfixed, lost in the wonder of the magnificent miracle that had occurred in the common, everyday garage.

After not too long of a spell, Eddie spoke.

"I would like to thank all of you kindly for bringing such a warm welcome to my fine pups," she said, holding her chin high with pride. "It pleases me immensely. But now, I must rest. It is very hard work to bring children into the world, and as yet I haven't had time to sleep." She curled up with her kittens, licked one of them on the head, and then lay her head down and closed her eyes. The room was silent.

Bonkers was the last to leave. As she was making her exit, she turned to see a light rain of shimmering sparkles floating down upon the sleeping family, covering them with an iridescent blue hush.

"Max," she said softly to herself, and walked outside into brightness.

All of the dogs stood around for a moment, blinking their eyes in the dazzling sunlight. Little yappy Aldo trotted back toward home. Orbit peered up into the sky.

"Holy chow chow! The sun has moved past the tall hemlock," he said with worry in his voice.

"Dog it—let's go," said Lula. "Gotta be back in the kennel before our people get home," she said quickly to Jack and Bonkers as she took off like a rocket.

Lula&Orbit raced up the street at top speed and rounded the corner to their kennel not a second before a car drove up and turned into their driveway.

"That was a close one," said Jack, now alone with Bonkers. He looked toward her and said, "Walk you home, pal." The two friends fell into step with each other.

"Jack," inquired Bonkers, thinking about the kittens, "isn't life magnificent?" The sight of the new kittens had overtaken her with great excitement and happiness, causing her to forget her woes.

He paused in his walking for a moment, and smiled. "Yes. Yes, it is. Definitely magnificent."

"They are such beautiful kittens," said Bonkers.

"You weren't here when Eddie was a kitten," reminisced Jack. "She used to climb all over Bear. She would sit on top of his head while he was sleeping, and he would never wake up until she covered his nostrils with her tail. It was hilarious."

Bonkers laughed at the thought.

"Yeah, Bear was a good friend. Did you know he was the one who taught Eddie how to speak Doggle?" asked Jack.

Bonkers shook her head.

"It's true. One day years ago, us dogs were hanging out up the street, and this little cat walks up to us and says, 'Hi, guys!' We were speechless—you might say the cat got our tongues."

Bonkers gave him an 'oh please, I've already heard that one' look.

"At any rate, my point is, it was Bear who taught Eddie. She kept climbing on his head, and that's when he taught her words. He said Doggle should not belong just to dogs; it should belong to whoever would make good use of it. He was a wise dog."

"Yes, he was," said Bonkers. She thought of Bear's teaching and his words, living on through Eddie. She thought about Bear and wondered where he was now and what it was like for him. "Do you think he is in a nice place?"

"Yes," said Jack with certainty. "Of course. I am sure of it."

Bonkers thought of Bear being in a nice place, warm and sunlit. He was free of cares, free of hunger, free of pains. She thought of his memories in the space she had reserved in her heart for him. *Incanninity,* she thought, reflecting on the Doggle word that meant roughly the same thing as the human word 'immortality.' *He lives on. Inside in our memories, through our repetition of his teachings, he is here. Incanninity. He lives on through those of us he has touched.*

Bonkers thought of life; she thought of death and of new life. She thought of how Bear's death was shortly followed by the birth of the new kittens. *Life never stops,* she thought. *It doesn't pause, not even to pay tribute to death. It simply goes on.*

"Jack—look," she said, pausing to look aside at a delicately beautiful spectacle: an egg sac just opening, with hundreds of tiny red spiders crawling out into the world. "Baby spiders."

"Yeah, I see," he said, peering closely. "Inky dinkies—and look how many. There must be hundreds of them. Maybe thousands."

Bonkers looked at the tiny translucent-red creatures, making their way out into the world, crawling on legs that were barely visible, thinner than hairs. She thought of how they would grow up to make their own egg sacs and create more spiders like them. She thought of how life kept renewing itself, and of what an amazing thing that was.

XV. A Vision

Rain pelted on the roof without relent, drumming steadily, like a torrent of little stones. The summer storm had spilled from the sky for weeks, unusual for the season but not unheard of in the rainforest. The deluge continued without a break or any sign of relief. It poured down on birds attempting to keep their nests dry with spread wings; it etched tiny rivers into the already soaked topsoil and found its unwelcome way into the burrows of mice and moles. It caused moss to grow atop the garden furniture, and it allowed mildew to thrive on anything wooden, its little black dots ever spreading. It brought with it a clammy, musty feeling that permeated people and caused them to check between their toes to ensure there were no little webs growing there. It made their skin look wan and pasty. It soaked the color from the world, making it dull and gray. It rained steadily; it rained without cease. It rained tadpoles and bullfrogs, snails and salamanders; it plunked and it drummed and it hammered.

Bonkers and Curtis James were obliged to entertain themselves indoors. JoelDad and MomSarah were absorbed by their respective computers, leaving the two junior members of the family to find amusement through their own devices.

"Bonkers, girl," asked Curtis James, "did you see Eddie's new litter yet?"

Litter? Bonkers wondered about the question. *No, I didn't see any litter there. Eddie is very neat, and besides, she must keep things extra clean with the new kittens around.*

"Livvy saw them," went on Curtis James. "She said there are five, the perfect number for a litter, and they are all very healthy. She said not one is a runt."

Bonkers deduced that her boy must have been referring to the kittens as litter. *Comparing living creatures to garbage? How odd humans can be,* she thought. *And the word 'runt' doesn't sound too nice either.*

Being somewhat bored by the eventless day, in addition to feeling a bit bothered by her boy's puzzling words, Bonkers felt a sudden urge to run. Run she did—out of the living room, through the entrance hall, through the dining room, skidding through the kitchen, sideslipping to turn the corner at the top of the stairs, fishtailing to turn at the bottom, past MomSarah at the computer, past the washroom, past JoelDad at the other computer, skidding into the fireplace doors with a slight bang as she turned, and then doing the whole thing again in reverse. Curtis James ran laughing behind her.

Bonkers raced faster and faster, her head bobbing frantically and her ears flying behind, her eyes bulging and wild, her tail low to the ground, her claws digging into the carpet or skidding on the floor as she turned. She ran like a wild dog, never slowing from flat-out full speed, narrowly missing table legs, running under chairs, and almost barreling into Curtis James; she always veered away at the very last second before she actually hit something.

The whole family stopped what they were doing in order to watch the show. MomSarah and JoelDad stood watching and laughing, and Curtis James yelled, "Go, dog, go!" as he attempted to run along with Bonkers, but ended up mostly having to jump out of the way of the speeding dog.

Bonkers, feeling more daring, zoomed faster and faster, coming perilously close to chair legs, walls, and feet. Closer and closer she came to collision, zanier and more reckless. *Nothing can hurt me,* she thought. *Nothing can stand in my way. Nothing can slow me down. I am a streak of lightning! I am invincible!*

Wham!Crash!Yipe!

Silence.

Complete, still silence. And darkness. Bonkers vaguely wondered why it was so dark in the middle of the day.

Curtis James rushed to the scene, followed closely by JoelDad and MomSarah. Bonkers had run smack into a wall. There she lay, looking quite like a squashed bug, her belly flat on the floor, her four legs spread straight out on all sides. She did not move.

"Bonkers!" cried Curtis James, tears coming to his eyes. Bonkers did not hear him, being in a far-off dream world.

Now it was no longer completely silent; distant, indistinct sounds, as if coming from afar, intruded upon her inner stillness, beckoning her to seek the source.

JoelDad knelt down by her to check her. "Her heart is beating," he said. He licked his finger and held it in front of her nose. "And she seems to be breathing okay."

"I'll get the car," said MomSarah.

Bonkers didn't hear the words being said, nor did she notice as her family lifted her and placed her on a blanket in the car. She had left Dirt for a little while, and she solely occupied the world inside her mind.

She was traveling, soaring through a sky afire with stars, crossing a great distance. She saw a planet ahead, opulent and beautiful. She recognized it instantly—it was the Dog Planet. She dipped down to it, looping over its mountains, gliding over its aqua oceans, skimming above its tall treetops, and sail-swooping above its sandy beaches.

Bonkers floated down to a gentle landing in a vast, sunny field, green with tall grass and speckled with bright wildflowers. The sky was a deep blue, deeper than any Bonkers had ever known on Dirt, and it was dotted by little white cotton-ball puffs of clouds. Down from this sky floated Max, alighting next to her. He moved his mouth as if speaking, but she could hear no words. She tried to speak to him, but all she could say was, "Mawa, Mawa, towa gindo ree?" It made no sense. Words would not form in her mouth.

"I have herecome to show-and-tell you," said Max, suddenly audible, intelligible, and clear-voiced. His coherence contrasted sharply with her ineffective gibberish.

She tried to ask what he had come to tell, but instead or words, out came, "Bwala, bloo?"

"Nuh-uh, Bonkers. You are not herebrought to talk. You are herebrought to listen up."

Bonkers, confused, sat and listened as Max sat tall and spoke his words clearly.

"*I am here to show-and-tell you about me.*" He spun about in a shower of sparkles, and then sat facing her again.

"*I am withinside of you,*" he stated firmly and with authority. "*Everyanythingallwhatsoeverwhich I did is inside you. Fast-tracking the way out of the forest after the thunderstorm, rememberizing the Mother Planet, resculeasing Lula&Orbit, fixiting the orange balloon-thingy, everyanything of it. It is allwhatsoeverwhich inside of you.*"

Bonkers, no longer attempting to speak, sat mute and wagged her tail.

"*I am inside you because I am a particule of you. You keepsake me there. Someone you love will eternalways be in you, for as long as you let them.*" Max began to glow and then rapidly became brighter, shining almost as bright as the yellow-white sun, except with more of a blue fiery hue. Bonkers' instinct directed her to turn away from the blinding light, but she now found herself curiously unable to move or even avert her eyes.

"*My bestest pal,*" said Max, "*I have a purpose on Dirt.*" He was now so bright Bonkers could no longer make out his form. All she could see was a bright ball of light.

"*I was put inside a fireball ship and sended down to Dirt to do something.*" His voice started to fade as the light he had become occluded all the surroundings. "*Something major big-deal.*" The grass, the flowers, the clouds, the sky—all was becoming overtaken by the brilliant sapphire light.

"*You will see,*" said Max's fading voice. "*You will all see,*"

As his words concluded, all vanished into brightness. All sound abruptly ceased, leaving only silence and brightness. Bonkers had to close her eyes to shield them from the piercing light.

Bonkers opened her eyes. She was somewhere else. She looked up and saw an unfamiliar white ceiling with a large, flickering, greenish fluorescent light. She felt a cold metal surface underneath her.

"Mom! Dad! Look!" She recognized Curtis James' voice and realized she was once again back on Dirt. She turned to his voice and saw his worried face. She turned to the other side and saw JoelDad and MomSarah. She tried to sit up, but her head ached so much she was forced to remain lying down.

Curtis James put his head down close to her face, and she happily licked him. The boy hugged her, and she drifted off into an exhausted sleep. She slept as JoelDad lifted her off the table, opened an eye as he put her into the car next to Curtis James, and went back to sleep. She remained asleep for the entire ride home. She woke as the car turned into their driveway and weakly lifted her drowsy, aching head.

There stood Jack, wet and bedraggled from the rain, waiting at her front door. He ran up to her as she was carried toward the house.

"I saw them carry you out and drive away," he said with concern. "Are you okay, pal?"

Bonkers was too weak and tired to answer, but MomSarah saw Jack and said, "Look—he must be worried about her. Let's let him inside."

MomSarah went to get a towel and rubbed Jack briskly to dry him. She placed a comfortable blanket for him to lie on next to Bonkers' pillow. The dogs were put in the living room in order for the family to keep a close eye on Bonkers until they felt assured she was recovering well.

Bonkers had a big lump on her head, a rather red left eye, and a throbbing headache. She slept as much as she could for the remainder of the day, which certainly felt better than trying to lift her aching head. Curtis James and Jack, true friends that they were, stayed by her side, while MomSarah and JoelDad constantly checked on Bonkers and brought treats and toys for the two dogs.

That night, Bonkers curled up with Jack beside the warm fire. She knew Max awaited her recovery: outside the nearest window she could see his sparkling glow.

In the middle of the night, Curtis James trudged sleepily from his room with a blanket and his pillow. Without making a noise, he gently curled up next to the two dogs and fell asleep.

XVI. Mischief, Mystery, and Blue Fire

By the afternoon of the following day, although still wobbly and not yet fully her old self, Bonkers felt just well enough to head outside on her own. The previous day had been the last day of the storm; it had finally passed in the night, revealing a soaked and glistening world. The sun shone warily, as if unsure of its permanency.

Jack had returned to his home early in the morning. He now came back to visit Bonkers with one of Eddie's kittens in tow, the one that was brown, white, and black. The kit was just barely four weeks old; too young to leave his mother for long, but old enough to search for adventure.

"Ow!" said Jack, as the kitten bit at his tail. Bonkers had to laugh.

"Those teeth are razor sharp," he said reproachfully.

"Ow!" said Bonkers this time, as the kitten pounced on her front paw with its perfect, sharp little claws. "Hey, you—knock it off." She carefully lifted the tiny kitten with her paw and tossed him up in the air so he landed, startled but completely unhurt, in some nearby bark dust.

The two dogs laughed, looking at the little kit that stood stiff legged and unsure of what to do next.

"Does Eddie have names for them yet?" asked Bonkers.

"No, not yet. She's waiting for their personalities to develop," answered Jack.

"That little fellow looks a bit like Max," said Bonkers, noting the similarity in markings and coloring.

"Leave it to Eddie to have a kitten that looks like an invisible dog," said Jack. He lifted his nose to the air and sniffed around. "Speaking of invisible dogs…"

Bonkers sniffed, and sure enough there was the smell of Max. The kitten turned tail and bounded off into the woods.

"I'd better go after him," said Jack. "Eddie would never forgive me if anything happened to him." He tore off into the woods after the kitten.

"Hey, old pal. How's sticks?" said Max, coming up behind Bonkers as Jack disappeared into the brush. "Ya feeling better yet?" He had visited Bonkers since her accident, but only briefly, during the few short times she had been allowed to go outdoors under supervision.

"Yes, thank you Max," she replied, turning to greet him. "It feels great to be outside." It was only as she turned toward him that she saw he was wrapped up in toilet paper all the way from his nose to his tail, appearing very much like a beagle mummy.

"Uh, Max…," she asked, "what are you doing?"

"Oh," he replied, looking down at himself. "Just a little bit of experimuttation." He blew a piece of toilet paper out of his face. "I guess it got a bit out of self-control."

"Max," said Bonkers, recalling her vision of the night before and wishing to change to that subject. "Can you hold off on your experiments for a minute? I have something I need to ask you."

"Sure think—just a minute," said Max. He spun around in a circle, going faster and faster, until he was transformed into a small blur of a tornado. Abruptly he stopped, and the tornado blur immediately transformed back into a sharply focused Max. There was no longer any trace of paper on him, and next to him a perfectly rewrapped roll of toilet paper toppled to a halt.

"Sorry about that eruption," he said. "You wanted to ask me a sixty-four dollar question?"

"Yes, I have many questions. Right after I hit my head, I traveled to the Dog Planet—it was as if I was having a vision or something—and you were there. You told me things."

"Like what?" asked Max, sitting and looking at her attentively.

"Well…you told me that everything you did is inside of me. And you said you are part of me."

"I did?"

"Yes, you did. And then you told me you have a purpose here on Dirt. And everyone would see. Do you know what any of this means?"

"Hmmm…," said Max, glowing slightly and starting to become transparent. "I don't know. Let me tiddlythink about it." His ears popped straight up in the air, his eyes bugged out, and his tail started spinning. It spun faster and faster until sparks flew in a crazy circle from its tip. His rear lifted up in the air a bit, and suddenly he shot electric helicopter-tail first up into the sky where he exploded into hot pink and fluorescent green fireworks. He reappeared from behind the smoke, floating back down to Dirt with the aid of a small parachute.

After he landed, he excitedly ran around in spark-trailing circles, and said, "Bonkers, it was like a philharmonica going off in my head! I have a purpose, I do—there's a rhyme and reason why I'm here."

"What is it?" Bonkers asked. "Tell me, Max."

Max attempted to slow his frenzy in order to think and speak clearly, but the wildness in his eyes betrayed the futility of his effort. "Yeah, yeah...okay...," he said, panting. He was very excited, so much that it confused his thinking and he became a bit lost in the head. "Okay. But wait; gotta put on my thinking map—I don't exactually know how to explain it, but—" Suddenly—poof—his head became invisible, revealing a small walnut-sized mass floating above his short neck.

"Max?" said Bonkers. "Max, where is your head?"

The beagle, oblivious to her question, answered with an excited voice that emanated from thin air. "First off, before I tell you my purpose, I have to tell you something really mega-important. You ready-set?"

"Yes, I'm listening," said Bonkers to the floating walnut-sized mass.

"Always keepsake a place for me in your heart," he said, "and I will always be there."

"Well, of course I will, Max," said Bonkers, not giving it a second thought. "I already know tha—"

Her words were interrupted by a zinging shower of sparks shooting out from a blindingly bright light where Max had just stood. Just as quickly as it came, the light disappeared to reveal...absolutely nothing. No trace of Max, no smoke, and no evidence of anything unusual ever having happened on this peaceful, sunny morning.

Another spectacular exit by the beagle, thought Bonkers. She did not dwell much upon the question Max had left unanswered—what his purpose could possibly be—because she was certain she would find out soon enough.

More pressingly, her head had once again started to ache, urging her to relax and erase all effort of thinking from her mind. She found a warm, sunny patch of ground where a small blue flower tickled her nose and stretched out.

That evening, Bonkers sat alone on the back patio gazing at the sky. The nearly full moon had just pushed above the horizon as the brightest stars emerged and the last rays of sunlight dissolved into deepening obscurity. At the edge of the woods Bonkers spied a large, indistinct shape that seemed to glide silently among the trees. She took a few steps toward it and peered closely, barely able to make out what it was. Suddenly she caught her breath—it was a deer, a young buck with a full head of antlers.

Breathless, she took another step toward him. Curiously unafraid, the deer left the cover of shadow and stepped out into the moonlight, walking toward her. He stopped, only a few feet from her. He stood stately and motionless, impressive majesty conveyed by his large silhouette. He looked straight into her eye with a calm, steady gaze. It was a gaze that, rather than imposing a challenge, suggested a certain gentleness, a quietude. And yet the animal's eyes also held the polar opposite—the energy and intensity of its wild freedom. What she perceived seemed different from what she had always felt inside of her, and yet there was something about it that was intrinsically the same.

That was it! That wild life inside the deer—it was the same life, the same blue fire she carried within herself. Bonkers kept her eyes locked in a deep stare with those of the deer, searching, insightful. She could feel electricity passing between them, and then she felt something strange beginning to happen to her.

Abruptly a feeling of intense awareness, as if it were a fiery maelstrom or the upheaval of a storm surge, swept over Bonkers. Opening herself to awe and wonder, she captured the firestorm as it hit. Ensnaring its intensity, she felt the blue-hot torrent of life: she felt life darting and surging through the world surrounding her; felt life climbing to the sky, exploring beyond this world; and felt life entering deep inside of her with each breath to run pulsating lub-dub through her veins.

If the dog and the deer were being observed, all would have seemed rather uneventful, most likely even dull. The two stood perfectly still, simply looking at each other. Nothing moved. All of the aforementioned maelstroms, firestorms, and torrents of life roiled deep inside of Bonkers, who experienced everything without even a twitch of her nose.

Brusquely, the deer broke the stare as if startled and lifted his head to the wind; the spell was broken. Brought back to earth, Bonkers lifted her nose and also smelled what had demanded the buck's attention: rapidly approaching rain.

Clouds moved in, obscuring the moon and stars; the soft nighttime glow disappeared as if suddenly erased. Lightning flickered and the wind picked up. As thunder rumbled, the startled buck broke to the woods for cover.

As fat, heavy raindrops splattered haphazardly around her, Bonkers, still feeling the wild electricity of the deer zinging inside her, tore home.

XVII. Wonder Dogs

Thunder rattled the windows as they were pelted by a barrage of angry raindrops being driven in gusts against them. Lightning illuminated the trees, frozen for split seconds in crazy, distorted positions as they were whipped by the wind. Rain poured down heavily and carried all the loose leaves and topsoil via suddenly formed rivers that instantaneously overtaxed the outdoor drains. The drains became clogged and rapidly overflowed; consequently, JoelDad, MomSarah, and Curtis James had to forgo the comfort of their beds to rush to bailout duty. JoelDad went out into the angry downpour and cleared debris from the drains so the water could flow freely, MomSarah blocked the water from entering the house and mopped up what was pooling on the garage floor, and Curtis James guided what was left out of the garage door with a squeegee broom.

It was hard dark-of-the-night work for the family, but soon the drains were again flowing freely, and all the water had been cleared from the garage. The storm continued to rage, but the three, satisfied with their accomplishment, were able to go back to their warm, cozy beds. Bonkers, who was always frightened by the thunder, had been waiting anxiously for their return under Curtis James' bed.

"Hey, girl," the boy called underneath the bed when he got back inside. "It's okay. It's just a little thunder. It can't hurt you."

Bonkers stuck her nose out just an inch and then cautiously emerged. Curtis James, yawning, patted her gently and she licked him. The boy climbed into bed and quickly fell into a deep sleep, while Bonkers remained awake, kept nervous by the noises from the sky.

Suddenly, Bonkers was startled by a horrifying noise from outdoors.

"GRRRrrrRRrrrRUUUR!! UrrRRRrrgrrrAAARRRRrr…" It was the angriest, most terrifying guttural threat from a dog that Bonkers had ever heard in her life.

In response came a low, "RRrrrrruuurrrrRuuurrrrrr…" This was not quite as loud as the first snarl, but with just as much, if not more, menace. Something about this one was more frightening, since it sounded somewhat doglike, but not completely. It sounded deeper, wilder.

Bonkers raced from under the bed, pushed her way through the broken screen, and ran out front to the street, from where the noises emanated.

A flash of lightning revealed a horrible sight: Max stood bravely in the middle of the road, menacing a coyote that held a precious treasure in its mouth—a kitten! Fear paralyzed Bonkers, cementing her paws to the pavement. There was a pandemonium of noise as a loud thunderclap mixed with the growling and snarling of the beagle and coyote.

The coyote looked huge in comparison to the tiny kitten dangling from its jaws. "Mew…mee-yew!" the kit cried in a tiny voice, just audible during the infrequent lulls of wind and rain. Bonkers recognized the kitten; it was the one Jack had been playing with earlier, the one that looked like Max.

Eddie ran across from her home, the terror in her eyes revealed by a strobe-flash of lightning.

The flash also revealed an altered Max, standing his ground with a fierce snarl, his ears pulled back, his hair on end, and his stance low and mean. He was a dog transformed; he was a fighter, feral.

Bonkers ran up beside Max, standing firmly beside him against the coyote. Eddie, tiny though she was compared to the coyote, stood with them, baring her teeth, hissing, and yowling with a mother's fury.

The coyote was unable to open its jaws to threaten loudly, lest it lose its prize, but it quite capably stood its ground, unwilling to give up its succulent feast-to-be.

"Let that child go!" snarled Max ferociously. "If you don't— GRRrrRRR—why, I'll—" His words were lost in another loud clap of thunder accompanied by deafening wind, shrieking with renewed force.

In between sheets of rain and dark, swirling branches, Bonkers saw shadows approaching, coming from all directions. A small flicker of lightning revealed the neighborhood dogs running over: Jack, Lula&Orbit, and even little Aldo. In the other direction, behind the coyote, there lurked an ominous shadow that looked rather like the form of another coyote. A small beam from a flashlight bobbed toward them from Bonkers' house, and at a slightly further distance, a light turned on inside Jack's house.

The newly arrived dogs joined in the standoff, uniting into one strong team against the coyote. Thunder rumbled through the air, mixing with the fierce growls of the comrades. Though they all snarled ferociously, they were reluctant to attack, for fear of it resulting in harm to the kitten.

"Bonkers! Dogs! What's happening?" frantically questioned Curtis James, as he ran up to the scene. When he saw what was happening, he stood in shocked silence, his mouth wide and his eyes filled with distress.

Bonkers looked as deeply as she dared into the terrifying eyes of the coyote, desperately searching their wild frenzy for some insight, some clue that might help. Then she remembered the steady stare of the deer and the vibrant intensity contained within his eyes.

Bonkers searched deeper into the coyote's eyes. There! She saw it—that fiery electricity she had seen in the deer, the one and the same vivacity of life she herself possessed. That coyote was not so different from her, nor from any living creature. That coyote had dreams, he had needs, he had ambitions and loves. He had fears.

Hmmm…fears, she thought. *…Maybe…*

"Max!" she shouted. "Remember in the Big Forest, when you followed the coyotes to their den?"

"Yeah, I memberize," said Max. "Hey Bonkers, let's amuse over this later—kind of busy right now."

"No, Max—listen!" shouted Bonkers. "I'll bet those coyotes were frightened off by your smell. Remember—how they ran away?"

Max thought for a minute, as snarls, screaming wind, thunder, growls, and lightning filled the air around him.

"Akita!" he yelled, with electricity in his eyes. "I eeny-meeny-miny-know what to do."

The dogs and the coyote remained locked in deadly standoff. Little Aldo ran in front of the other dogs and yapped with as much fierceness as he could manage in the face of the big coyote. The wild animal looked down at the little dog with amusement, as if he might consider having a meal of little-yappy-dog instead of succulent kitten.

The coyote's amusement didn't last long—it was quickly replaced by terror as he raised his head to see a bloodcurdling sight.

Max had mutated—his head was grossly enormous. Dazzling fireworks and black smoke shot out of his ears. His eyes were as large as saucers, bulging with red veins and bugging out of their sockets. His razor-sharp teeth had grown large enough to engulf the entire coyote with one swift snap.

The coyote's fear rendered him incapable of moving. That was unfortunate for him, because the worst was yet to come.

Max opened his giant mouth, and forced out his bad breath. Only now it was no longer ordinary bad breath; it had mutated beyond Max's usual malodorous halitosis. Far more ghastly and rancid, it was now a blistering blast of repulsive stench. It hit the coyote full-face with the force of a hurricane. The wild animal was engulfed by an odor far more noxious than any to which it, or any living creature, had been previously subjected. Added on top of Max's already powerful putrescence were all the foul-smelling forces of his collected treasures: the stinking rotting slugs, the decomposing peaches, the moldy decaying food, the rotten egg, the mildewy rank wads of dubious biological origin, the reeking stink bug, the funky skunk effluvium, the festering garbage—every miasmic, awful, noisome, grimy, asphyxiating, putrid thing he had put in his mouth since he had so long ago arrived on Dirt. All magnified, all mutated to a level of stench beyond any previously known on the planet.

The coyote dropped the kitten. It tore tail between its legs YIP-YIP-YIIIIPE! off into the woods. It was closely followed by a dark blur that Bonkers guessed must have been another coyote. The kitten, unharmed and not the least bit bothered by the smell that now covered him, ran to Eddie, who smothered him in licks.

The other dogs and Curtis James stood sputtering and coughing, unable to escape the permeating stench, even in the pouring rain.

Just then, Livvy arrived on the scene, trying with difficulty to see through the windy, rainy night. She gagged a bit from the fumes, and she pinched her nose tightly shut. Other flashlights could now be seen, coming out from houses along the street.

"Max, you did it!" cried Bonkers. "You're a wonder dog!"

Standing alongside Max during the standoff, the other dogs had not recognized him for who he was. Now that the danger was over, they all turned to stare at him.

"Max?" said a dumbfounded Jack, staring at the beagle. "Bonkers' invisible friend? Of course—I recognize your smell, at least in the usual less concentrated form—but I definitely recognize it. But look—now I can also *see* you."

"Holy mongrel! You're real," said an astonished Orbit.

"The bravest, smartest dog there is!" said Lula, with stars in her eyes.

"And the kindest," purred Eddie, as she and her kitten rubbed up against him. "I can never thank you enough."

"Take a bow-wow," said Jack.

"Awshucksgollygee," said Max, his nose twinkling bright red.

Aldo wagged his tail and licked Max's paw. Curtis James and Livvy stood speechless, wide-eyed despite the pelting rain, amazed and very happy. The flashlights that had recently emerged from the houses came closer.

"Bear would've been proud," whispered Bonkers into Max's ear.

All speaking at once, the dogs rapidly bombarded Max with questions:

"Where do you come from?"

"How'd you do that gonzo monster-head trick?"

"Why do you stink so bad?"

"How come we couldn't see you before and now we can?"

"How'd you know how to scare off a coyote like that?"

"Why do you glow?"

"Whoooooa doggies!" shouted Max. "All these question marks are rattling inside my head and confuddling me. Please sit down and listen up."

Bonkers sat down at his side, and the other dogs assembled in a captivated circle at his feet.

"Okay," said Max exuberantly, "it makes me very hap-yappy you can see me. It makes me even more happy-go-puppy this here little guy is still with us." He nuzzled the kitten.

"There are so many things I want to show-and-tell you," continued the beagle. "More wonders in the universe than you can shake your tail at, oodles of poodles of secrets right here on Dirt, a corgicopia of delights on myour home, the Dog Plan—"

ZZZZAP! Before Max could finish his words, he was engulfed by a blindingly bright sapphire light as a great thunderous noise shook the ground under paw and foot. Suddenly there was no Max—hovering just above the spot where he had stood was instead a great flaming boulder, lighting up the night as if it were daytime. Before anyone could get a second look, the meteorite, for that was what the boulder of a sudden proved to be, shot straight up into the air, into the sky. The blazing meteorite blasted through the clouds, breaking a gaping hole in them as it rocketed through. Great billowing trails of cloud shot upward, following the electric-blue fireball toward the infinity of the night heavens.

Since the clouds overhead had been cleanly blasted through, the rain abruptly ceased. The wet world below glistened in the light of the meteorite, as it arced into sky toward the stars. As the adults from the neighborhood began to arrive, they gaped upward at the sky. Although diminishing in size as it ascended, the meteorite remained brilliant and spectacular, clearly visible through the hole it had created. Its trail was reflected in all the upward-looking eyes—all that is, except Bonkers' eyes. Those remained curiously jet-black, as if the light and energy were absorbed right into them.

Several hushed and amazed murmurs from the stunned adults, mingled with the surrounding quiet: "What on earth...?" "What could it be?" "It's like some kind of reverse meteorite...I guess..." Livvy scrambled to Jack, and Curtis James ran beside Bonkers.

Bonkers looked at the charred spot on the ground where Max had stood. Glinting on the ground was something small, shiny, and golden. She took a closer look and saw it was an upside-down pin. She flipped it over with her nose and saw a dog peering at the stars through a sextant— her gold navigator pin from the Dog Planet! She picked it up carefully in her mouth and brought it to Curtis James.

"What's this, Bonkers?" he asked. As he examined it, he said, "Look, it has a dog on it—and the dog is using a tool...looking at stars. Neat. You wanta wear it, girl?"

Bonkers barked happily and sat at attention at her boy's feet. Curtis James pinned it on her collar. Bonkers wagged her tail, and then looked up at the sky. She said, "Max," more with pride and amazement at his great feat, than with sadness at his departure. She knew he was still there, inside of her, in a place in her heart. She also knew, she could feel it, that at some future time she would once again see him in the fur.

"Max," quietly repeated the other dogs, as they gazed upward.

"mmmm...mmMax!" said the kitten, speaking his very first word of Doggle.

All the animals turned to stare at the little kit, but only briefly, for the clouds were regathering over the hole caused by the meteorite, and the rain was starting up again. Adults collected their children and pets and ran to their respective homes, attempting to escape the downpour that was resuming with added fury.

At the edge of the woods, a lightning flash revealed not just one, but as Bonkers had suspected, two coyotes standing, looking back at them.

Another flash a split-second later revealed that the wild animals had disappeared, vanishing into the night. Bonkers looked up to catch a final glimpse of the meteorite ascending into the starry sky, just before the clouds abruptly closed behind it.

As soon as the clouds did so, there was a blinding flash of lightning, and a colossal crash of thunder that violently shook the entire street and the Woods-in-the-Back. Bonkers, her eyes wild with a new energy, one of cosmic lightning and feral tempests that added even more intensity to her already zip-zing intrinsic blue fire, ran to her beckoning family. Pelting rain, thunder, wind, and lightning chased them home.

XVIII. Life Is a Treasure

Peace had returned to the Woods-in-the-Back. The initial cleanup of fallen branches and debris was performed swiftly, and the weeks following the storm were carefree and lazy. These were the last few weeks of summer, the languid time before the dutiful bustle of autumn. It was a time to lie in the grass and find animals in the clouds, or to dangle feet over the edge of the tree house, or to blow bubbles bigger than your head. It was a time when the leaves were fat and dark green, and the breeze was soft and warm.

The kitten that had been rescued from the jaws of the coyote had taken to following Bonkers home. He often curled up next to her for his nap, purring himself to sleep while Bonkers licked him. She enjoyed his company; whenever he came around, she felt like a little bit of Max came with him. In fact, at times she was nearly certain that the smell of Max followed him, as if the odor had become an entity that had attached itself to him.

One day, Curtis James happened upon Bonkers lulling the kitten to sleep, and he went to get JoelDad and MomSarah to see. They watched quietly, so as not to disturb the sleeping friends.

"How sweet," said MomSarah.

"They're a good pair," said JoelDad. He and MomSarah looked at each other for a few moments, and then they both nodded. MomSarah went inside to make a phone call.

"Well, Curtis James," she said when she came back out, "what do you want to name him?"

"You mean he's ours?" asked an incredulous Curtis James. "Our very own? One of the family?"

"Yessir," said JoelDad. "One of the family."

"Oh, boy!" shouted Curtis James, forgetting all about the fact that the two furry friends were sleeping. He quickly clapped his hands over his mouth. Bonkers opened a drowsy eye, but the kitten was too lost in sleep to be roused.

Curtis James sat down to think carefully about an appropriate name for the kitten. After a sufficient period of reflection, he stood up.

"I like Ringo," he announced. "It's a good boy-cat name, and it makes me think of rings and treasure. After all, treasure's what he is after his rescue."

"Then Ringo it is," said JoelDad.

Bonkers, careful not to disturb the sleeping kitten, gave a wag of approval, and it was settled.

There were happy times ahead for the family, as they welcomed the new member into their group and got to know him. Ringo was very playful; he liked just about everything, and he made a game out of just about anything. Every morning, when Bonkers licked Curtis James' hand, Ringo jumped on the boy's head to awaken him. He crawled into anything in which he could fit, and tugged on everything he could reach. He pounced on every person, animal, or thing that moved. He chewed the heads off yellow rubber duckies, which were quickly put out of reach again, and he rolled himself up in toilet paper. He was unstoppable in his playful energy.

There was, however, one unfortunate thing fate had handed to the kitten: the odor of Max. Bonkers was not the only one who noticed it had transferred to him. MomSarah bathed Ringo often, shaking her head in bewilderment as to how such a small kitten could constantly get himself so horribly stinky. Luckily, the good-natured kitten, in contrast to just about every other cat in the world, liked baths.

On the last afternoon of summer, Curtis James tumbled in the grass with Bonkers and Ringo. The boy laughed as the kitten pounced on him. Bonkers sneaked up behind Ringo, gently lifted him with her nose, and tossed him up into the air. The kitten recomposed himself, and then ran after Bonkers in mock anger. Bonkers was far too swift for the short-legged kitten to capture, and Curtis James, watching the spectacle, rolled in the grass with laughter. Ringo, unable to even touch Bonkers, turned his attention to the boy and pounced on him.

"Help! Help! Save me, Bonkers," called Curtis James, pretending Ringo was ferocious.

Bonkers just sat down and observed with amusement as the kitten tumbled atop her boy.

"Hi, pal," said Jack to Bonkers, as he trotted over from his yard. Ringo quickly changed his attention from Curtis James to Jack; he jumped off the boy and ran over to tug at the terrier's tail.

"Whyyy uuuu little…," said Jack, as he rolled onto his back and twisted his body to bare his teeth, jokingly of course, at the kitten.

"Wh...wh...why!" whispered the kitten, almost inaudibly.

Bonkers laughed. "It sounds like somebody's ready to learn some more Doggle."

"Why?" said the kitten again, this time a little louder.

"Because," said Jack, with all seriousness, "you are displaying desire and readiness."

"Why?" asked the kitten once again, this time with more strength and confidence in his voice.

"Because it's time," said Jack, growing impatient with all the 'whys.'

"Why?"

"I don't know. Because the sky's blue," said Jack shortly. "Just because."

"Why?"

"What are you, some kind of 'whys' guy?" asked a flustered Jack. Ringo had a good laugh at the result of his teasing.

"Okay now, you got that out of your system?" asked Jack when the kitten was done laughing. Ringo sat down and looked attentively at Jack.

"Good. Now let's get started. Follow me." Jack headed into the Woods-in-the-Back. The kitten bounded after him, every once in a while taking a swat at his tail. "See ya later, pal," Jack called over his shoulder to Bonkers.

As the two entered the woods, Bonkers could hear Jack's fading voice. "Now, the first thing you need to learn about is Tidbits and Scraps. They are the only words in the human language you need to..."

Bonkers and Curtis James were now alone. The boy found a tennis ball, and threw it as far as he could for his dog to chase. She tore across the lawn, her gold navigator pin gleaming brightly in the sun, and jumped twisting into the air, catching the ball on the first bounce. She sat down on the spot and dropped the ball, and Curtis James laughed and ran to get it and throw it again. Over and over, the boy retrieved the ball for his dog. The two friends spent the remainder of the afternoon in throwing, catching, tumbling, running play. When they were breathing hard and the shadows grew long, they lay down beside each other in the cool grass and looked between overhead leaves at the reddening sky. Bonkers recalled Bear's final howl: *Warm dirt, inviting sun. Heaven.*

"Look—," said Curtis James, pointing with a blade of grass on which he had been chewing, "the first star." Bonkers could just make it out, peeking from behind breeze-ruffled leaves and branches. A pensive look passed over the boy's face and he said, "I wonder where your beagle friend could be."

That's where, thought Bonkers. *On the Dog Planet, just beyond the brightest star—that star.*

Bonkers stretched and lazily scratched her back on the soft grass, and then she lay perfectly still. She sensed without moving the eternal turning of the world, a firefly dizzy-whirling nearby, the stars beyond traveling through infinite blackness. She sensed the infinity of life embracing her and her boy, enveloping them.

She licked Curtis James on his nose, and he laughed.

About the Author

When she was still an impatient and discontent teenager, Mignon bought a standby ticket and packed a single suitcase. She left her home and an Ivy League education behind to stubbornly pursue her own path on the opposite coast.

After several years of mucking about in all kinds of boring, miserable jobs in which she put things together the way other people wanted them, she decided to go to art school and make things her own way. Art school was exciting and fun, and she earned a BFA in photography. Upon graduating, she learned a creative education does not necessarily lead the way to a creative career; she operated a desktop publishing business and found herself using her new skills to once again put things together the way other people wanted them.

Currently, Mignon C. Reynolds uses a keyboard for her creative outlet and lives in the Pacific Northwest with her husband and son. She likes it there.